Praise for *Fir*

'A wonderfully imaginat
packed and full of heart. P(
fairy tale characters lived in modern day ....

—Alexandra Sheppard
author of *Oh My Gods*

'A unique and magcial book filled with familiar characters, but re-imagined in a whole new and exciting way.'
—Tọlá Okogwu
author of *Onyeka and the Academy of the Sun*

Finding Folkshore

Rachel Faturoti

JACARANDA

This edition first published in Great Britain 2023
Jacaranda Books Art Music Ltd
27 Old Gloucester Street,
London WC1N 3AX
www.jacarandabooks.co.uk

A CIP catalogue record for this book is available from the British
Library

ISBN: 9781913090920
eISBN: 9781913090937

Cover Design: Rodney Dive
Typeset by: Kamillah Brandes

To Tobi, because I can't not dedicate the first book I ever wrote to you.

Chapter 1

'FOLAAAAAAAA! *OMOWAFOLAAA*! Ò nìí pa mí
lónìí!' Mum screams. *You will not kill me today!*

I can tell when she's mad because her Yoruba starts
showing. Can I ever get any peace in this house?

'I'm coming, Mum.' Turning back to the mirror, I try to
style my afro. It's summer so my hair's on a break from weaves
and braids. My hair-care ritual is long. I did all the heavy
lifting last night with the shampooing, conditioning, parting
my afro into sections and twisting it. The end result is a twist
out. As I take my hair out of the twists, black curls bounce on
my dark brown skin.

'Fola, come out of the bathroom!' Mum shouts. 'What are
you doing in there? Why must it take you so long?'

'Mum, I'm coming!' I open the door to find Mum and Bisi
waiting outside.

'You're actually wasting my time,' Bisi moans, trying to
push past me into the bathroom.

I screw up my face at my sister. 'What are you smirking
at?'

'I'm laughing at that mop on your he—'

1

I don't let her finish as I swat her ear. She cries out.

Dad emerges from his bedroom, frowning. 'Ah ah.' He's dressed for work in his smart trousers and 'strong' shoes, as he likes to call them. Dad's shoulders are so wide that he takes up more space than me and Bisi put together. 'Stop fighting. Bisi, you need to learn how to respect your elders. And Fola, stop hitting your sister. You better hurry up and get dressed if you want to drive with me.'

He shakes his head and stomps off. My dad teaches at my school, which I'm still not used to. I don't like it, but what am I supposed to do?

After buttoning my white shirt and tucking it into my pleated grey skirt, I shrug on the ugly green striped blazer which, after, like, 50 years, *finally* fits me. Mum always said I'd 'grow into' the uniform, but tell that to 12-year-old me. It's been *four* years! My skirt used to swing around my ankles. As if I needed anything else to make me stand out at that school.

I fix my hair in our full-length mirror, loving the way the tendrils fall around my face like a flower blossoming. Lifting up my camera, I turn my head at different angles and take some pictures in the mirror. Should I start my own channel about hair? Yeah, no. Forget that! I'll just get drowned out by all the other people online.

Once I'm done, I follow the sweet smell of yam and egg down the narrow corridor. Sometimes I swear this house feels too small for the six of us, but at least it's bigger than our flat in London. I guess moving to Kent wasn't that bad—actually no, it is, as I'm still sharing a room with Bisi. My older brother Deji and my younger brother Roti get their own rooms because my parents said Deji is 'too old' to share. He's only nineteen—three years older than I am.

The walls of the orange corridor are covered in plaques of Bible verses. The 'As for me and my house, we will serve the Lord' one is always crooked, and this makes sense because Bisi is a pagan. I stop at Deji's closed door. It's odd him not being at home, but I definitely don't miss hearing him groaning in pain at night.

I wish there was something I could do for him, but there isn't because I'm not a doctor. Slouching down in one of the Ikea kitchen chairs, I yawn loudly. 'I'm hungry, Mum. Is the food almost ready?'

'Come and finish these eggs. Where are Rotimi and Bisi?' Mum asks as I pull the spatula from her overworked fingers.

I stab at the scrambled eggs and whisper under my breath, 'How would I know? I'm not Google Maps.'

Mum's head turns like a handle, and I know she's heard me. Even if I was standing on top of Mount Everest whispering, my mum would still hear it all the way from Kent.

'I'm your mother, not your friend, Fola! I never spoke to my mother like that.'

'Okay, okay. Mum, I'm sorry.'

Mum leaves the room and Bisi swaggers in like a lioness with no care in the world: youngest child syndrome. Her 18-inch Brazilian weave settles softly on her right shoulder as she drags out a chair to sit down. The weave is from my aunt, and now my aunt's wallet is crying.

Meanwhile, Roti is going through an awkward stage with his gangly body like a grasshopper. One minute I was looking down at Roti, but now he's looking down at me. As Roti enters the kitchen, he mumbles 'morning' to me before serving himself food. Once he's done, I dish out yam and egg for myself, taking a seat next to Roti at the glass dining table.

'Aren't you gonna serve me?' Bisi asks. She even has the nerve to give me a dirty look like I'm her slave.

Turning around, I look over my shoulder to the left and then the right because Bisi must be talking to someone else.

'Your legs aren't broken,' I reply mid-chew. 'Serve yourself.'

Roti sniggers so hard that a small piece of egg goes flying out of his mouth towards Bisi, making her shriek.

'Let's pray,' Mum says as she enters the kitchen. She gives Roti the eye to drop his fork and we all bow our heads. 'Thank you, Father, for allowing us to see a new day and for the food we're about to eat. I want to pray for healing for Deji. Heavenly Father, make the cancer in his body disappear, in the name of Jesus. I know his health is in your hands, Heavenly Father, and I pray the surgery goes well.'

'But if Deji's health was *really* in God's hands, then why's he sick?' Bisi asks. 'You pray so much, but why isn't he better?'

See. Pagan.

I can feel Mum's glare from where I'm sitting. *Here we go.*

'God, I'm asking you...' Mum's head flies back and her mouth twists as her words attack like missiles. 'Kí ni èṣè mi tí olorun fi funmi irú ọmọ báyìí?'

What did I do to deserve a child like this?

4

She narrows her eyes and points a calloused finger at Bisi. 'Why are you like this, Adebisi? I didn't come to this country for this.'

Bisi's glare matches Mum's. 'We get it. You and Dad came to this country from Nigeria with nothing.'

Roti chokes on a piece of yam, which he'd slid into his mouth when Mum started shouting. If I spoke to Mum like that, the only thing being shipped back to Nigeria would be my body.

'What is going on here?' Dad bellows from the doorway. 'Stop it! We are a *family*.'

'Yeah, sure we are,' Bisi scoffs, getting up from the table and slamming the front door on her way out.

'If she continues, I'll send her back home. Let her try that rubbish there,' Mum warns and storms out of the kitchen.

Roti scrapes his chair back then grabs a container to empty his breakfast into. Whistling, he swings his bag onto his shoulder. This is a normal morning for us.

One hand grasping his keys and the other holding his brown, worn briefcase, Dad says, 'Let's go, Fola.'

After taking one big bite of the yam, I grab my bag and meet them outside. It's always the same. They fight *all* the time.

The door to the family's Toyota creaks as I settle into the passenger seat, Roti behind me. Dad switches on the radio to the news and I zone out.

We drop Roti off at St Michael's Secondary School. Bisi's probably laughing it up with her friends on the bus. If she's late to school again, everyone in the house will hear about it. I can't even *think* about being late to my school.

Dad continues on to St Joseph's, passing decent-sized houses and modest cars. Slowly, the houses become mansions with long driveways and brand-new Mercedes-Benzes parked outside. St Joseph's grand steeple peeks out above the mansions. With its lush green grass and winding trails, it's my sanctuary—and prison. I can't lie, though. It's great that I got in because it's one of the best private schools in the UK, but I feel like I'm carrying Mum, Dad, and my family in London and Nigeria on my shoulders. My grades got me in and gave me an Academic Excellence scholarship because I'm really good at school. They think I'm some sort of maths prodigy. What can I say? Maths is my boyfriend and Pythagoras's theorem turns me on.

I get my love of maths from my dad. He teaches now, but I remember how he struggled to get qualified. Dad was a university lecturer in Nigeria, but he had to retrain in this country. I know that Mum hates her job at the residential home. It wasn't easy at all for my parents in the beginning, and I remember all the times we ran out of electricity. Deji and I help out where we can, but the focus has always been on our education. This adds even more pressure because if I don't succeed then my parents went through all that for nothing. Sometimes I wish I was average, and then they wouldn't expect as much from me.

The creak of the handbrake forces me out of my head. Dad sighs and his fingers drum repeatedly on the steering wheel. I wonder if he's remembering his life back in Nigeria. Dad used to tell me about his friend Nneka and how they used to fetch water together in the village. I feel like he regrets coming here sometimes, but I know my dad: he'll never say it because he's all about family.

The outside of my private school looks like 20 mini castles joined together to make a mega castle. Priya waves at me from the entrance as all the Jacks, Olivers, Daisies and Rachels swarm past me into the main building, creating a blinding platinum sea mixed with shades of browns and reds. I already know someone's annoyed Priya by the way her foot's tapping. Priya swings her long brown hair over her shoulder and fluffs her bangs.

'Fola. I'm tired,' she moans. 'Ahmed is *so* inconsiderate. They already took my room, so I have to stay in that *tiny* guest room, and now Abdul won't stop crying!' She throws her hands up in the air. 'I mean, I love his chubby cheeks, but he doesn't let anyone sleep.'

Priya's brother, Ahmed, is refurbishing his house so he, his wife and their new baby have moved back home for a while.

'Hi to you too,' I reply. 'Yeah, it's so cramped in your six-bed house.' I roll my eyes. 'I don't know how you're coping.'

'I swear. If one more person comes into my room without knocking...'

It makes me think of the day I met Priya. Brad was being rude to her, so she cussed him out in English and then in Bengali. It was beautiful, really.

She grabs my shoulders and shakes me until I snap out of my daydream and notice her.

'Fola. FOLA! Are you even listening to me?'

'Yes,' I answer. 'I'm listening. Were you wearing your period pants?'

I move away quickly as she tries to hit my arm. 'I'm sorry.' I laugh.

She pinches me. 'It's not funny! It's so embarrassing, man. We're going to sixth form next year, which means we're almost proper adults, and I still have to tell people to knock. Come on!'

'No, *you* come on.' I pull on her hand. 'We're gonna be late.'

Entering the school, we stop at the bottom of the polished wooden staircase. It has a blue carpet running down the middle like a tongue. Students move around us in their uniforms, mini-mes of their socialite parents. The interior screams old money with its grand arches and high ceilings. And you should see our canteen! With curved bronze doors, multiple serving stations, solid round tables and stained-glass windows, it feels like I'm eating in a palace. Our library looks like something from the future, as the books go around on a carousel. We even have our own chapel, theatre and swimming pool. I can't even swim, but still.

Once we get to the landing, I walk up the staircase to the right and Priya to the left. My triple science biology class is filling up, and I head to my seat at the front. The atmosphere crackles with tension: we're in the top set and we have to do well.

'Quickly, take your seats, please.'

Mrs Newman strides to the front in her standard black suit and blue loafer combo. Her vintage blackboard on wheels rolls in behind her; she refuses to use the smartboard and prefers to go old-school. As the chalk hits the blackboard, we all pray. Mrs Newman is strict but fair.

BODY REGULATION

'We shall see who has been paying attention. Mr Jones, come up to the front and explain to the class what thermoregulation is and how it works.'

Roger slowly rises from his seat and makes his way to the front, his mouth moving quickly as he tries to remember.

'Thermoregulation is the control of the internal body temperature, and it works by...'

Mrs Newman nods as Roger explains exactly how thermoregulation works.

'Thank you, Mr Jones.' She points. 'You may take your seat. St Joseph's will make a fine biologist out of you yet.'

Through her half-moon glasses, Mrs Newman scans the room, and we all shrink a little in our seats.

'Ms Oduwole,' Mrs Newman says. 'Where is the hypothalamus located and what does it do?'

God, why? Seriously. Dragging my eyes back to

Mrs Newman's crossed arms, I hear thankful sighs as I get up—a fallen soldier.

'The hypothalamus is an area in the brain...' I explain something that I looked at for, like, two minutes last night because I was too busy working on a new short film idea. 'And it regulates body temperature.'

'Correct,' Mrs Newman states.

The 'correct' is as dry as the chalk in her hand.

'Katherine, you're next. What does vasoconstriction mean?'

For the rest of Mrs Newman's lesson, I'm half working, half watching the clock. As the bell sounds, she gives us homework. 'Please go over pages one to ten for our next class and I expect to see you all in the extra revision session.'

We all pile out of the class with the weight of our approaching GCSEs on our shoulders. Only three months away!

'You all look miserable,' Priya mocks from the wall outside the classroom.

'Whatever, man,' I reply. 'It was a good lesson. Mrs Newman showed us this video on temperature regulation, and I got an A on a test we did.'

'All I heard was "good lesson".' Priya shrugs and starts heading towards our form room. 'I find science dull.'

I rush to catch up to her. 'And you say *I* don't listen. It doesn't matter anyway. Look who's coming.' I spot Mukesh walking towards us, and I grab Priya's arm. 'Pree. Seriously. Be easy, okay?'

'Good morning, my Indian goddess.' Mukesh stops right in front of Priya and gives her a wonky smile.

'No,' Priya states. She dodges him and continues down the corridor as if his pride isn't lying on the floor.

'Yes!' He pumps his fist. 'I'm making progress. Yesterday she told me to take a running jump off a cliff.'

'Sure. Keep telling yourself that,' I mutter, patting him on the shoulder.

I run after Priya's retreating form as she enters the blue archway. All students belong to a house, and these are known by their colour. The houses are named after people who have achieved greatness. Pankhurst House is green, Einstein House is red, Franklin House is orange, Chaucer is yellow and we're in Seacole, which is blue. I love being in this house because Mary Seacole was a British Jamaican woman who set up the British Hotel during the Crimean War.

As I sit down in my seat, Millie turns around to me. 'I love what you've done with your hair, Fola. I've been trying to get my hair to be wavier, but it's just bone straight. I'm jealous. What's your secret?'

My right eyebrow rises. 'It's my natural hair.'

'Oh, but last week you had straighter hair. My friend Yemi told me that it's a weave.'

She whispers the word 'weave' as if it's a secret. I stop myself mid-eye roll. 'Yeah, it was *still* my hair.'

Sometimes I feel like the spokesperson for all black people because there are only two of us in my whole year. I get new hair anxiety because I know people must comment when I change my hair.

Oh my gosh, you've changed your hair.

How did you manage to get it straighter, curlier, shorter?

I prefer the other hair on you!

I didn't recognise you.

I'm the only black girl in this form.

Ms Jackson, our form tutor, drops her bag at the front and whistles. 'Listen up. I've read all your statements and given some feedback on them. Please go over my notes and amend ahead of our practice interviews on Friday.' She whizzes around the room, giving out the statements for our interviews with St Helen's sixth form. It's my statement of lies.

I want to study further maths, chemistry and biology for A level because I've always wanted to be a doctor...

But what I truly want to study is film, photography and maths. It's not the whole clichéd 'she's applying for the boring subjects, but really wants to do the artsy subjects' story. Or the 'her parents won't allow her to be herself, but in the end she breaks through all the barriers and becomes her own person' story.

Well, actually, it's *exactly* that.

Deji is lucky because he chose a science degree, which is on my parents' approved list of degrees. I can choose from the long list of doctor, lawyer or accountant, but I've always felt like my camera was part of me. I'm the designated family photographer, probably because my parents are cheap and don't want to hire someone professional to do it.

It all started when my parents took us back home to Nigeria.

If I close my eyes, I can picture my first time meeting Nigeria. I was ten years old. The dry heat surprised me as we walked out of the airport in Lagos. All of my senses were drawn in. Young boys in mismatched clothes were trying to sell phone cards outside the airport entrance, but they parted as my uncle Tunde rushed to meet us in his old black BMW. We shoved our luggage into the big boot, then we all squeezed into the back, and we were off.

Lagos was loud and larger than life. It was like an open zoo, with chickens and goats crossing the road. People weaved in and out of each other like bracelets, and noisy okadas sped past my window carrying passengers.

When we reached the city of Ado Ekiti, I met my dad's family and they told me all these funny stories about Dad when he was younger. Apparently, he was always getting into trouble. I couldn't imagine it.

Using Dad's Polaroid camera, I photographed lots of things, from a beautiful navy-blue Ankara dress with yellow swirly patterns to a lizard scurrying across the compound, leaving a trail of dust in its wake.

But in Nigeria, I also saw the gap between the rich and poor. It was like looking into two different worlds. From then on, I wanted to inform and educate through my films. I want to be known everywhere for my films, but that'll only ever be a dream because I'm going to be a doctor.

Ms Jackson's voice pulls me back into the room. 'It's important that you choose subjects that align with your future careers.'

My phone vibrating in my pocket interrupts Ms Jackson's speech. Priya eyes me as I check my phone.

Deji

> They're moving me to London today for the surgery.

My heart sinks.

Chapter 2

While I watch my container of jollof rice spin around in the microwave, Priya taps her foot impatiently on the canteen's shiny hardwood floor.

I ignore her.

'So, what was that message about?' she asks. 'It's fine if you don't want to tell me.'

Here we go.

She tuts. 'Okay, actually it's *not* fine.' Priya turns to stare at the side of my head. After a few seconds, I throw my head back and shift my body to face her.

'If you have a secret and you're not telling me, Fola—'

'It was from Deji.' I sigh.

Priya puts her hands up to stop me. 'Say no more. Why don't we sit outside and blind these peasants with our awesomeness?' She balances her hot container in her hand, while I put mine back into my plastic bag.

The scent of spices trails behind us as we walk down the corridor to the grassy area around the back of the building.

'I can't wait for our theatre trip to London tomorrow,' Priya squeaks, cutting her roast beef into small pieces. 'OMG, I'm sorry, Fola. I forgot. I've got such a big mouth.'

Deji's surgery is the day after our trip. I've known about the surgery date for months. I've been dreading it because it's risky. They need to remove a tumour from his spine.

'It's alright.' I stop playing with my jollof rice. 'Pree, sometimes don't you feel like there's so much pressure on us to be the best?'

'Every single day! I can hear my nani now.' With her eyes narrowed, a thick Indian accent and a wagging finger, Priya channels her grandma. 'Preeeya, don't disgrace us.'

I burst out laughing. 'Why are our families so dramatic?'

'Don't you remember? My dad had a heart attack when I told him that I wanted to be a writer. There was a whole family meeting.' Priya points her fork at me then eats the beef. 'You should've seen my auntie shaking her head in the corner. My uncle asked if I thought I was Shakespeare or something. I was shocked that he even knew who that was.'

I take a bite out of my chicken and just shake my head. The rest of lunch flies by. We quickly pack away our stuff as the bell rings.

'Byeeee,' Priya sings, reaching in for a tight hug. She steamrolls her way towards her geography lesson, while I make my way to the art block. My second home.

I can breathe easy there. My parents still don't know that I chose media studies for a GCSE because they were distracted by all the other 'serious' subjects I chose. If I ever told them what I really want to do for A levels, they'd *definitely* have a heart attack.

I can imagine Mum now. *Fola, do you want to kill me?*

As I push open the mahogany door, people are shouting and laughing. Gregg, our media studies teacher, blows a large golden horn at the front of the class.

I jump forward. '*The Lord of the Rings!*'

'Darn! I knew that one.'

'I was going to get it.'

'Who even watches that stuff any more?'

Gregg points the horn at me. 'You got it, Fola. In *The Lord of the Rings*, the Horn-call of Buckland was used in times of danger or battle.' He blows the horn again. 'Get in your pairs. You should all have an idea of what you want to do, or should have started your projects. Before I forget—Fola, Ronnie, Nora and Paul, can I speak to all of you quickly?' Gregg motions to the front of the class.

What does he want to talk about? I know I'm not failing media studies because it's the only subject I put effort into. Once we reach his desk, he hands us each a flyer.

CHARLTON UK FILM FESTIVAL
presents

SHORT FILM COMPETITION
for BAME filmmakers aged 18 and under
Any theme
Win a **£1,000** prize
A chance to show your film at the
International Film Festival
Win a paid summer internship in a film studio

I take my time absorbing all the information before responding to Gregg, but Paul beats me to it.

'Do you think we have a shot?' Paul asks curiously.

'Yes, I do.' Gregg speaks with such certainty that I almost believe him.

Me? Entering a film contest? Nah. It's a waste of time. What would my parents say?

Gregg watches us. 'Please, can you all do me one favour? Can you at least think about it? If you need a crew, I know some people who would love to help out.'

Ronnie's wavy black bob bounces as she nods her head. 'I'm going to enter, and I have the *perfect* short film to enter with. When we were vacationing in the south of France last year, I shot some footage.'

The south of France? The only south I've been is south London. It must be nice to not only have money, but also parents who support you.

Folding the flyer three times so it's small enough to stuff into my blazer pocket, I move back to my seat, but Paul stops me and asks, 'So, what do you think?'

I push a curl of hair out of my face. 'I don't think I have time to do it.' I shrug, like my dreams aren't folded up in my pocket. 'Because of school and all that. You know how it is.'

'Yeah. Same,' Paul agrees. 'My parents have been on at me about getting all As.'

'Tell me about it,' I mutter.

We go back to our seats, but I can't stop thinking about the competition. Imagine if I won. It would change *everything* for me. My parents won't worry that I'll end up working in Odeon.

For the rest of the lesson, I try to listen to what Paul is saying about camera angles, but I can't concentrate. Would you be able to?

The end of school can't come quick enough because I can forget about school and see Deji in the hospital.

I climb into Dad's car and he takes off, without a word, to pick up Roti and Bisi. Mum is meeting us there. Usually, Dad would attempt some small talk about school or something funny a student did in one of his lessons, but he's probably not feeling it, and neither am I.

'Family,' Deji says jokingly as we walk into his hospital room. 'What did I do to deserve this visit?'

Sitting on the edge of his bed, Deji balances his long feet on the last empty chair in the room. He's 6 foot 2 and complains that everything is too small for him.

It's still strange seeing Deji in the hospital. He's always been active—going skydiving, rock climbing, mountain biking and surfing. I throw up on the teapot ride at the local funfair. Deji swore all of us to secrecy about him skydiving. If Mum found out he'd purposely jumped out of a plane, she would lose it.

I push Deji's legs gently until he moves them with a cheeky smile.

'Move, man.' I flop down into the chair. 'What do you think this is?'

'Hello to you too, sis. Still drowning in that green blazer, I see,' he mocks.

Sticking my tongue out at him, I reply, 'Still skipping leg day, I see.'

We start laughing while Mum complains about how disrespectful I am.

'Hey, bro,' Roti exclaims, spudding Deji with his fist.

Bisi is chilling in one of the other chairs, on her phone, pretending we don't exist as usual.

'What exactly did the consultant say, Deji?' Dad asks. 'Is everything scheduled?'

'Yup. They're probably scared to do the surgery here because they don't want to risk having a dead black boy on their hands,' Deji jokes.

Mum clicks her fingers. 'I reject death in Jesus' name!'

'I'm only joking, Mum.' Deji groans. 'It's a fancy specialist centre.' He turns to me with a smile, but it doesn't look as bright as it usually does. 'You should see their facilities, Fola. They even have a rehab centre in case I have to learn how to walk again.'

'You can't joke about these things, Deji,' Mum scolds him.

The rest of us are silent, thinking about all the possible complications of the surgery. I know that he's scared. We all are. Who wouldn't be? I knew it was bad, but learning how to walk again?

Mum pats Deji's hand. 'God is in control. He won't let *anything* bad happen to you. We should pray for you and the surgery.' Mum bows her head, waiting for us to do the same.

'God, I want to thank you for everything you've done for Deji...'

The prayer goes on for 20 minutes. I say my own prayer in my heart because the surgery *has* to go well. My brother has to be alright.

'Ameeeeen!' Mum rounds up her prayer and stands up with a deep groan. 'My darling boy. It is well.'

I know the nurse will be here soon to tell us that visiting hours are over. There's a flurry of movement as we say goodbye to Deji.

'Wait a sec, Fola,' Deji says, pulling on my blazer.

Deji waits until our family has left the room before he speaks again. 'You alright?'

'Yeah, I'm cool,' I reply, playing with my hair. 'It's just...'

'I know all of this is hard, but all you can do is focus on the positive.' He shrugs. 'That's what they keep telling me. God's got me—he won't let a good one die.'

I grin. 'Yeah, you're right.'

I lean down to hug him, and the folded-up flyer falls right in his lap. Hospital or no hospital, his reflexes are still *way* quicker than mine.

'What's this?' he asks, smoothing out the flyer.

I reach out to snatch it back. 'It's nothing, okay.'

Deji ducks under my arm and reads it. 'You better be submitting a film.' He stares at me. 'Fola, were you not gonna enter?'

'No. I don't even know what I would submit,' I reply. 'Why are you looking at me like that?'

'Because I know for a *fact* you're working on something right now. I know you don't wanna hear it, but your short films are sick, and you have all these ideas. Just think about submitting. Promise me.'

'Fine. I promise that I'll think about it.' I take the crinkled flyer back, staring down at it.

Chapter 3

The thick red curtains close and the dim lights flicker on, lighting up the dark theatre. People from my form leave the theatre to get snacks or use the toilet.

'Intermission is only 20 minutes,' Ms Jackson calls. 'Make sure you're back in here by then.' After ticking her 'good teacher' box, she wanders off, staring *way* too hard at her phone.

I take out my phone and message Deji back. They're taking him in for final tests before surgery. 'Whatever it is, Pree, I don't want to do it.'

Priya huffs. 'If you really don't want to know, I won't tell you.'

'Alright.'

Priya's tapping foot matches the key tones on my phone. *Here we go.*

'There's this night tour at the British Library...'

'No.' Pocketing my phone, I look at my friend to make sure she's for real. 'We're not going to no night tour.'

Priya throws her hands up in the air and looks sulky. 'You don't even know what I was going to say.'

Wait for it.

Priya continues, using a softer tone. 'Fola, it's not even like that and it's not *technically* a night tour. Remember when we were getting snacks earlier? I met this group, and they were talking about this fun game. So...' She rummages through her small black Chanel bag, bringing out two tickets and wiggling them in my face.

Pushing her hand away, I give her a look that says 'are you completely out of your mind?' and 'you better not be serious'.

'They're gonna use you as inspiration for one of those true crime Netflix series,' I say. 'I'll give a good interview about the type of crazy friend you were. I'm not going, and *you're* not going. Priya. Look at me. We're not going.'

'Pleeease, Fola,' she begs, grasping the front of my jacket. 'I promise you it's going to be fun. You never want to do anything fun nowadays. You're always talking about school.'

I lean back. 'What are you trying to say?'

Priya sits back, tucking her bag in her lap. 'Forget I said anything. We don't have to go anywhere. You're right.'

I touch Priya's shoulder to get her attention. 'No, you were gonna say something. Just say what you were gonna say, Pree.'

Sighing deeply, Priya plays with the gold chain on her bag. 'It's just that you've been *very* stressed lately.'

What is Priya talking about? We're *all* stressed trying to get good GCSEs—and my brother is sick too. Clamping my lips together so I don't say anything rude, I let Priya finish what she was going to say.

'And like,' she says quietly, 'I completely get it because of what's going on with your brother, but I miss my best friend.'

'Alright,' I snap. 'We can do this night tour then. It better be good.' I get up from the cushy red chair and don't even wait for her as I stalk out of the dim theatre. She catches up with me a second later and loops her arm through mine. Leaning into me, Priya whispers, 'Trust me. You're going to love it.'

I better, because apparently I'm no fun anymore. *What's that supposed to mean?* Yeah, sorry I'm not chatting about shopping when my brother is sick, and I need to focus on school. Priya's rich. She doesn't have to worry about all the things I worry about. If she fails, she has her family to catch her, but I don't want my parents to have to catch me.

Five minutes later, we're standing outside the British Library with Priya bouncing in excitement.

The 'tour guide' waits outside the gates. Her cropped blue hair matches her fur coat perfectly. If I'm cold, then she must be freezing in that short quilted skirt, but who am I to judge?

'Welcome to the British Library night hunt!' she bellows, dancing around like she needs the toilet. 'A night of thrill, games and fun!'

'How are we even allowed in here?' I ask Priya.

Pree shakes my arm in excitement. 'I'm not telling you because you'll ruin it. Fola, just relax. Your parents aren't here and Deji is *fine*. You've messaged him, like, 20 times already.'

Blue Hair explains the rules of the hunt. Each team gets a map and the first team that can solve all the riddles wins.

Priya pulls me so we're at the front of the line. Entering the library, our footsteps echo across the near-empty building.

As she drags me up the wide steps, the library is a white blur until we come to a large, well-lit room. It's an exhibition on the art of storytelling. We're not the only ones here. There's a group of teenagers around our age hanging around the room.

A petite black girl with a red pixie cut and a nose piercing speaks to her friend. 'Ty says that we're all snakes for not bringing him in.'

The tall, slender girl beside her with deep brown skin and a septum piercing replies. 'Who cares what he thinks, Red?' She rubs her shaved head. 'You know *exactly* why we couldn't tell him. We're not even supposed to *be* here and I thought you broke up. You act so dumb cos of him sometimes.'

Red screws up her expertly contoured face and arches her shaped eyebrows. 'Don't chat to me like that. I'm not one of your likkle friends, Rapunzel. Remember that.'

Rapunzel?

What kind of name is Rapunzel? Isn't she the one with the long hair from the Disney film?

Rapunzel bristles like teeth on a comb. I don't realise I'm staring until Rapunzel's chestnut brown eyes meet mine, and she screws up her face like I'm battered plantain.

Turning away from her, I touch Pree on the shoulder, ready to start this tour. 'What's the first clue?'

'Uh.' She fumbles with the paper, then stares at it for a

few seconds with her bottom lip sticking out. The paper is upside down. This girl has no idea what she's doing.

Leaving her to fail, I move around the displays. Special spotlights reflect off the glistening glass and small summaries detail the history of storytelling. Opposite me, a white boy in a black hoodie is talking on his phone. He has an Irish accent.

'But why didn't they tell me that Noah was going on a trip, for Christ's sake?' He scowls, pulling his hood down further. 'It took me *ages* to get back into London. I've been trying for months.'

I move over to the other end of the room, where there's the tallest book tower I've ever seen. Like a snake, the book tower bends and spirals upwards, almost touching the ceiling. How are the books not falling?

I'm so distracted by the book snake that I bump into someone. Pale, tattooed hands shoot out to catch me before I fall. It's the boy in the hoodie.

'Steady on, lass. Where's your head at?' he asks jokily.

The hood falls away to reveal a white boy around my age and height with icy blue eyes, a crooked nose, and long blond hair pulled into a low bun.

Priya senses cute boys like sharks smell blood in the water. As if by magic, she materialises beside me before the boy can finish his sentence.

'Yeah, Fola.' Pree giggles. 'Don't get too close to the books or you might fall in and end up in Folkshore.'

The blond boy freezes, like his eyes.

'Folkshore? Where's that?' I ask.

'Are you joking, Fola?' Priya laughs. 'How can you *not* know about Folkshore? Didn't your parents ever tell you not to stick your nose in a book or you might end up there?'

It feels like the whole room is listening to our conversation now, including Red and Rapunzel, who are staring at us. *What's going on?*

Priya is completely oblivious as she focuses on the paper, now right-side up.

Red tries to whisper to Rapunzel, but her voice is loud. 'Did that girl just say Folkshore? How does she know about us?'

What is it about this Folkshore place that has everyone shook? It's not even real.

'She knows. We go back. Now!' Rapunzel growls at her friends. 'I *knew* it was too risky coming here.'

What do they think I know? A whiff of Lynx with a hint of cigarettes hovers in the air as the blond boy bows to Rapunzel. 'I guess the queen's spoken. Us mere mortals shouldn't worry her about anything as minor as seeing their families.'

Rapunzel storms off. Her black Docs pound against the floor as she marches out of the exhibition.

Red moans and calls after her friend. 'But we can't go yet, Rap. I still haven't been to Oxford Street, and you know my birthday is soon.'

The blond boy whistles loudly and follows, the rest of the group behind him. Why are they acting so strange?

'Fola. Where are you going?' Priya asks. 'Fola! Are you listening to me? The tour isn't over.'

Priya can keep on solving riddles, but I'm going after the others. Something's not right. *Why are they in such a hurry to leave?* As I exit the library, I keep the strange group in my sights.

'Seriously, Fola. Where are we going?' Priya asks, running behind me. 'Is it somewhere fun? It better be, because I paid almost £50 for that night tour.'

'There's something off about them,' I reply. 'When you mentioned that Folkshore place, the girl, Red—you know, the one with the red hair—was worried because you mentioned it. They think I know something, Pree and *that's* why they left in a hurry.'

Priya jumps in front of me, blocking my path. 'You mean we left a fun tour to chase after some strangers because of some imaginary place? I have to go back to screaming Abdul tomorrow, and we're doing this?'

You know when you can feel something is off?

'Pree, trust me. It's *me*. How many times have I followed you places? Remember that time I forged your dad's signature?'

'Which time?' Pree laughs, because I've done it many times.

'You're the one who said I'm always talking about school,' I whisper. '*You* said I wasn't *fun* anymore. I just have a feeling.'

Priya was right about me changing. I want to do

something spontaneous and not think about the conse-
quences or my family.

'Alright but only for you, Fola and because I love spying
on people,' Priya says. 'I don't mind following that cutie in the
hoodie. Did you see his tattoos?'

We follow the group down into King's Cross station. A
jittery feeling fills my chest. The group are laughing and
jumping down the escalators, except Rapunzel. Pree and I
hide under one of the arches at the Victoria Line platform
so they can't see us. Train after train goes past, and they still
don't get on. *Was I wrong?*

'See, there's nothing strange going on. How long are we
waiting for?' Priya asks, putting her phone away. 'Robbie said
Ms Jackson is asleep, so we're okay. Are we going to talk to
them or not? I can talk to the blond boy.'

The jittery feeling disappears and I try to hide my disap-
pointment. 'Yeah, we should go back. I don't wanna get in
trouble.'

One of the skaters from the group shouts down the platform. 'Yo, Prince!' He points. 'The next train to Brixton is
ours.'

There's been, like, 50 trains going to Brixton. *What's so
special about the next one?*

The blond-haired boy reappears on the platform and
gives him a thumbs-up.

'OMG, did you hear that? His name is Prince,' Priya
gushes, her cheeks turning pink. 'It's perfect.'

As the train arrives and the doors fly open, people rush out and the group get on further down.

'What's so special about this train?' I ask Priya. 'We should get on.'

'And go where?' Priya moves closer to me. 'I only agreed to follow them here, Fola. It was fun, but I'm not following some strangers onto a train.'

The beeping sound of the doors is a bomb waiting to explode in my head.

'Is this because of what I said before?' Priya asks. 'I didn't mean it, Fola. Honestly.'

'It's not about my family, Deji or s-school,' I stutter. 'I just... I just have a feeling, you know?' I shout, before jumping onto the train.

The doors slam shut.

The last thing I see before we go inside the dark tunnel is Priya, standing on the platform. *What did I just do?*

Chapter 4

I rock forward in the seat. The dark tunnel blurs, and so does my brain, as we speed to the next stop. The jitters are a distant memory. My stomach tenses. *What are you doing, Fola?*

I can't believe I followed strangers onto a train because of a feeling. I should've stayed and finished the stupid night tour with Pree then snuck back into the theatre.

'The next station is Euston. Doors will open on the right-hand side. Change for London Overground and National Rail services.'

I'm getting off.

As I stand by the doors, my gaze strays to the strange group in the next carriage of the train who are laughing it up. Seriously, though. Where are they going?

Prince turns my way and I quickly look down. The train comes to a sharp halt at Euston, and a blast of wind hits my face as the white doors fly open to a packed platform.

'This is Euston. Change here for London Overground and National Rail services. This is a Victoria Line train to Brixton.'

'Excuse me, are you getting off?' a woman asks from behind.

Am I getting off?

Others become impatient and push past me with loud grumbles. I move out the way to let the woman pass. 'No, I'm not.'

Sitting back down, I cling on to the bar as we speed to the next stop, but I keep the group in my sights. I don't try to get up again until we reach Brixton.

'This is Brixton, where this train terminates. All change, please. Change here for National Rail services.'

My carriage empties, but I'm still sitting down because the group are there talking. Why aren't they getting off? A London Underground worker gets on the train in a hi-vis vest, with one of those grabber things and a clear bin bag. He bobs his head aggressively to the loud rock music playing in his wireless earbuds, his dirty blond ponytail swinging from side to side.

He blocks my view of the next carriage. 'Are you reading that?' he shouts.

I lean back.

After seeing my face, he removes one of his earbuds. 'Sorry, mate. I forget these are in sometimes. Are you reading that?'

He points to the *Metro* newspaper lodged under my bum. I didn't even feel it. Plucking it from under me, I hand it over to him and he dances down to the next carriage.

I get phone signal for a second, and all Priya's messages come through at once.

Priya

> Are you having a midlife crisis? A teen crisis?

> My Aunt Mariam ran off to India to become a goat farmer.

> Is it like that?

> I'm trying to call you.

> FOLA!!

As I begin typing a message back to Priya, the doors beep again then slam shut. What's going on? The engine fires up and the train speeds off down the track. Where are we going?

As the train lurches forward, I'm thrown to the floor. Jumping up, I bang on the train doors, trying to pry them open with my fingers. My heart tweaks, matching the speed of the train. I should've gotten off! Mum's going to kill me. The police will show up at my house, and she'll drop to the floor because she thinks she's in a Nollywood movie.

The low, squeaky whine of the carriage door opening has me reciting every single Bible scripture I know. The carriage door clicks shut, and I hear soft footsteps come closer to me.

'Excuse me, miss,' someone croaks behind me. 'Can I see your ticket, please?'

As I whirl around, the scream I was going to scream gets stuck in my throat and I shakily grab the bar. *What the hell?*

Starting from his polished black shoes, I look up, taking in his scaly lime-green legs with the faded dark spots and his creamy bulbous stomach stretching the forest green train conductor's suit. Holding out his webbed orange hand, he opens his mouth again. 'Miss, please can I see your ticket?'

As he blinks, a clear piece of skin covers his bulging eyes.

I scramble backwards and trip over my feet. 'Don't come near me!'

A frog. A talking frog dressed like a human. Where did he come from?

The carriage door slams shut and Red comes up behind the frog train conductor. 'Leah! There you are,' she says, looking at me.

Confused, I frown. 'Leah?'

The frog conductor's head tilts and his bulbous eyes assess Red. I bet he's picturing us as juicy flies.

Red hangs off my arm like we're besties. 'Your memory is so bad, man.' She stuffs a ticket into my hand. 'I was holding your ticket for you, re-mem-ber?'

I look down at the hexagon-shaped purple ticket. I can tell it's fake because, while the ticket is faded, the letters look brand-new.

From
KING'S CROSS ST. PANCRAS
To
LONDON FOLKSHORE
<<<ONE WAY>>>

But the conductor doesn't seem to notice. He plucks the purple ticket from my fingers, stamps it and places it back in my hand. 'Thank you, miss. Looks like another storm is coming into Folkshore tonight.' He tips his hat. 'Have a good evening, kids.' He moves through to the next carriage. It's as if everything rushes through to my brain at the same time, like a flood.

'Folkshore? Storm? Frog?' I whisper. 'Nah, I'm done. I must be dreaming.'

Red clicks her fingers in my face. 'Then yuh better wake up.'

'How do I get back to King's Cross?' I ask.

'You can't,' Rapunzel says, appearing through the carriage door followed by the rest of the group. 'Why did you follow us?'

What does she mean I can't? I need to get back to Pree and Deji. I need to get back to the normal London.

Rapunzel's slender jaw is clenched so tightly that it might shatter. She hits the window, pissed. 'I knew we shouldn't have gone. What are we gonna do with her?'

Her? Me? Who is she talking to like that?

'My name is Fola, and you don't have to *do* anything.' I blow up. 'Just show me where I can get the train back.'

Rapunzel's eyes narrow. 'Are you stupid? I said you *can't*.'

Red shakes her head, looking tired of Rapunzel's rudeness. I'm tired of it too and I've only just met her.

'What's your problem?' I ask.

'The next station is Folkshore,' the announcer says.

Prince whistles. A cigarette is perched in the corner of his mouth. 'What can ya do?' He shrugs.

We're approaching a purple, oval, glass building with octagon pieces on the outside. The bullet train loops around the circular platform, making my stomach flip before coming to a screeching halt.

'This is Folkshore station. Please mind your paws, legs, fins and claws.'

I move mad *once*—just once—and now I'm here.

Someone pounds on the window behind us. A human man glares at us from outside. He's in a blue security uniform and has a walkie-talkie chilling in his belt. As his fingers twitch to reach for it, Prince swears under his breath.

'Can I see your identification cards, please?' he asks.

Pulling up his hood, Prince turns to the group. 'Feck. Keep your faces hidden and leg it.'

As if they're in some kind of action movie, Prince, Rapunzel and the rest dart off the train and rush down the platform.

The security man dashes after them. 'Stop, now!'

It's only Red and me left on the train.

'Come on, we're going this way,' Red says, jumping off the train.

Shrugging on my hood, I rush after Red like a headless chicken, as Mum says. I can imagine her asking: 'If your friend jumped off a cliff, would you jump?' At this point, I would, Mum, because I'm stuck in this mythical place with talking animals and people with names like Rapunzel, Prince and Red.

'Why aren't... we going... with them?' I ask in gasps as my legs pump down the glass platform.

'Because security is going that way. Do you wanna get caught?'

Red gives me a look and I give her one back because no one is getting caught today. It feels like we're running in circles. The circular platform doesn't help, but we finally get to a flight of stairs. Red stops at the top.

'Where is it, man?' Red asks, feeling around the glass panelling. 'I swear it was here.'

'What are you looking for?' I ask.

'Don't just stand there gawking.' Prince appears, out of breath. His tattooed hands move across the middle of the panelling until he reaches the centre.

The glass panelling opens to reveal a dark opening with steps going down.

'Thanks, Princey baby.' Red pats Prince's cheek and descends into the darkness.

Rapunzel barges past me and follows Red in. *What's her problem?* And where did the rest of the group go?

'They went the other way. Ya really need to sort out that

thinkin' out loud thing.' Pulling out a torch from his bag, Prince points the light down so I can see. 'In ya go.'

This, right here, is how I die.

My foot hits the first step as I descend into the darkness. My Converses hit the ground. Red and Rapunzel have already started walking down the tunnel.

The Chronicles of Folkshore. At approximately 7.45 Folkshore Standard Time, an unidentified person enters Folkshore with a black bag on their back. This unidentified person is called Fo—

'Who said that?' Where did that come from? The chronicles of what? 'Did you hear a voice just now?'

'Watcha on about? I didn't hear a peep.'

This place is making me hear things now. *Am I losing it?*

Laughing, Prince answers the question that I swear I asked in my head. 'Doncha know all the best people are potty?'

As we move further down, the tunnel trembles and tiny pieces of rock shower down from above.

Rap stops, frowning up at the ceiling. 'What was that?'

'There's a storm brewin', ' Prince replies. 'We gotta move a wee bit quicker or we might waken a Shrieker.'

'What's a Shrieker?' I ask.

'Shriekers don't exist,' Rap barks. 'Ignore him.'

Prince chuckles at that, making spooky ghost noises as we walk down the dark tunnel. At the end, there is a set of stairs spiralling upwards. Prince climbs them carefully, then opens the steel door. We're thrown forward into the station as the ground trembles violently. I'm scared the glass pods positioned around the station will shatter into pieces.

As a loud alarm blares through the empty station, we run towards the exit. The lights flicker, and rain pelts the building. Reaching the automatic doors, we fight against a powerful gust of wind, which almost blows us away.

The tornado engulfs the station, but we don't stop running. I thought the station was weird, but Folkshore itself looks like something out of a fairy tale. The luminous trees have winding twigs like sparks of electricity, and they join together in the middle from either side of the street, but not all the trees are luminous. Some are dark.

A strange tickling sensation works its way up my throat, and I sneeze, but the sneezing doesn't stop. Red hands me a tissue to blow my nose.

'Thanks,' I say. 'I dunno what that was.'

Rapunzel gives me another dirty look, like I should die quietly. Even though it's dark, the pastel-coloured cottages stand out. Pretty Victorian-style lampposts are positioned along the street. Only some of the lampposts house an orb of white light; the rest are empty. Why haven't they changed the light bulbs?

We reach a junction with all these funky street names and a stocky black boy—who's definitely one of those gym heads—jogs across the street towards us, his hench arms protruding out of his black boiler suit.

'Hey, Westley.' Red wiggles her fingers at him.

Westley grins, flashing a friendly smile. 'You alright, Re—'

Stalking towards him, Rapunzel cuts him off with a rant about me. 'Can you believe this girl followed us here? If the pigs find out, it could ruin *everything* we've been planning against the Assembly.' She takes off down Goblin Grove with Westley running to keep up with her.

'Bye to you too!' Red shouts after Rap.

A faint whistle travels in the wind. Prince turns around and spots the rest of the group from the train further down the street. 'See ya.'

It seems like everyone is getting collected except me. Red heads down Goblin Grove, seemingly expecting me to follow.

'Where are we going now?' I ask, tired of being dragged around.

'Greenwood.'

Yeah, I'm not going anywhere else until she tells me exactly where we're going. 'What's Greenwood?'

Red sighs, looking up from her phone. 'My man's aunt manages the place, so you can sleep there tonight, unless you wanna sleep outside. Tomorrow we can find another way to get you back.'

'But didn't Rapunzel say I can't get the train back?' I reply as my head throbs.

'Look.' Red holds up two almond-shaped red nails. 'You have two choices: stay here or come with me.'

After a few seconds I nod, because what else can I do? I'm

stuck in this strange place because I decided to follow them onto the train. I should've stayed with Priya.

After walking further up Goblin Grove, we turn onto Knight's Lane. Red stops in front of a vast cottage with arched windows and a curved roof with a small yellow flag waving. A large sign rests on the top: *GREENWOOD—Giving teens a refuge.*

Red holds a card against the door and it clicks open. Once we're inside, I follow her up the beige-carpeted stairs. We enter an open space that has multicoloured bean bags, a ping-pong table in the corner, and an L-shaped sofa. The 85-inch flat-screen TV mounted on the wall is so much bigger than the one we have at home.

Home.

What is happening there now? Mum's probably crying on the floor and begging the police to find me because I've been kidnapped. Dad is trying to calm her down while Bisi is laughing at me in her group chat. Deji will be smiling because he thinks I'm off doing something 'risky', and Roti will be chilling by himself in the corner—eating and observing the madness.

Taking out my iPhone, I try to call Priya, but the number is unavailable and the messages I send to Deji don't go through either.

'You won't be able to call or text anyone out of Folkshore, because they're not on the approved list,' Red says, rolling her eyes. 'It's annoying.'

'You have an approved list for numbers?' I ask. 'Can I use your phone then?'

'They brought in the approved list after the Reckoning,' Red replies. 'Sorry, your numbers won't work on my phone either.'

'The reckon what?'

'The Reckoning, and Rap was right,' Red says as we climb up the stairs. 'You *really* shouldn't have followed us here. This place is messed up, man.'

I wish I hadn't either.

'If you meet me at the library tomorrow, I can try and figure out another way for you to get out.' Red pauses outside a closed door with the name 'Maleficent' on it. 'You ready?' She curls her fist and knocks.

'Ready for what? Wait, wasn't Maleficent the evil witch?'

'It's open!' someone shouts from inside.

Is Red bringing me to be sacrificed or something?

Red goes into the office, but I don't move. The door is wide open, though, so I can see a sturdy black woman, with a short curly brown weave, sitting behind a desk.

'Hey, Mal,' Red greets her.

'Red. What are you doing here so late? You here to see Ty?' She wags her finger. 'Remember my rules about late visits.' A deep crease appears between her eyebrows as her gaze rests on me. 'Who's this?'

'Oh, this is Leah. My cousin.'

Her what?

Chapter 5

Peeling my eyes open, I stare around at the beige and white room, remembering exactly where I am. I rub at my itchy eyes. 'Achoo!'

My socks sink into the white carpet as I get up to draw the light curtains. The oddly shaped multicoloured buildings of Folkshore fill up the skyline. I wish this was all a bad dream.

Today is the day of Deji's surgery, and we're *all* supposed to be there. I can't miss it, and I definitely can't stay here. Last night, I couldn't even sleep because of the storm, and the words from the voice kept repeating in my head.

The Chronicles of Folkshore. At approximately 7.45 Folkshore Standard Time, an unidentified person enters Folkshore with a black bag on their back. This unidentified person is called Fo—

Let me deal with the fact that I'm hearing voices later. One problem at a time, Fola!

Maths and biology, I can do, but this? I can't do none of it. Throwing on my clothes, I check my phone again, but there's still no signal and the time is 7pm. *Why hasn't my time changed?* The wooden clock above the bed says it's 10am.

The door creaks as I open it, sticking my head out to make sure the coast is clear. Hugging my bag to my chest, I follow the signs to the bathroom, creeping down the first flight of stairs. I twist the metal doorknob, but it's locked. If it was Bisi waiting outside, she would've been complaining, even though she takes over an hour to get ready.

'I'm comin'!'

Through a thick cloud of smoke, there's a curvy white girl with long, raven hair piled on top of her head in a lopsided bun. Her ears are covered in piercings, including the helix one that I've always wanted. When I told Mum I wanted to get it done for my 17th birthday, she started begging me in Yoruba not to move over to the 'dark side'.

'You're Leah, right? Red's cousin,' she declares, watching me out of emerald eyes. 'Me and your cousin don't really get on, you know.'

I can't believe Red lied about me being her cousin from another part of Folkshore. Mal made her call 'my mum' to check if I could stay at Greenwood and 'my mum' agreed over the phone. I don't know which woman was pretending to be my mum over the phone. If my real mum was on the phone, she would've broken into Folkshore and dragged me out.

'Achoo!' I sneeze and rub my eyes.

'I think it's something in the air,' the girl says. 'I was sneezing and coughing up a bloody lung when I came to Folkshore. You might feel a bit weird too, but it goes away after a while.

I never really knew what it was. Oh, and my name's Branna, but you can call me Bran.' She smirks. 'See you around.'

The hot water from the shower steams up the bathroom and I hunt through the toiletry bag Mal gave me for a toothbrush.

'Fola, you're gonna get out of here today,' I say to myself in the mirror. 'No one can stop you from getting home except yourself.'

I pull the comb through my afro and flinch as it gets caught in a tight curl. A bumpy high bun it is—it's never tight enough, anyways.

I shower quickly and leave the same way I came. There are framed photographs of Greenwood's directors and trustees. Mal's photo is up there as the director of Greenwood, and the photo beside hers is of a man called Rumpelstiltskin Gold. He has the most hypnotic golden eyes. They *can't* be real.

Rumpelstiltskin Gold
a former resident of Greenwood and director.

'When I became homeless at the age of thirteen, Greenwood was my refuge, and I'm positive that it will be a refuge for others too. To some, my upbringing is regarded as unsavoury, but it was a foundation for greatness and success.'

The previously empty common room area is now full of teenagers. I ignore everyone and lean on the wall, pretending I don't hear them talking about me.

'You cool, Ty?' A light-skinned boy in a red T-shirt spuds Ty, a tall black boy with skin slightly lighter than mine.

Isn't Ty Red's boyfriend?

With his grey tracksuit, silver chain, fresh black Air Force 1s and a shape-up as slick as his smile, I see why Red's with Ty.

'What's good, Sebastian?' Ty replies.

'Did you hear about the stop and searches?' Sebastian asks. 'The pigs are looking for someone who came into Folkshore last night.'

I came into Folkshore last night.

'Swear?' Ty tilts his head. 'I hate them. The pigs are always about for no reason.'

'Leah,' Mal calls out, drawing even more attention to me. 'Sorry, but I need to move our meeting this morning. I have an emergency.'

That's even better because I can find a way out of here without someone asking questions. 'That's cool.'

'I swear you're Red's cousin,' Ty says to me after finishing off his conversation with Sebastian.

If Red didn't tell him the truth about who I am, then I'm not saying anything.

'Yeah, something like that.'

I'm consumed in a strong perfumed hug by Ty, which I'm too slow to dodge. 'We're basically family then.'

'Nephew,' Mal says to Ty. 'Let me talk to you for a second.'

Someone turns up the volume on the TV. All attention is diverted to the screen where a tall, slim East Asian woman with thin eyebrows, straight brown shoulder-length hair and rosy lipstick stands outside Folkshore station. Scaffolding and plastic sheets hide the station from view.

'This is Anna Tsang here, reporting live from outside Folkshore station. Late yesterday evening, a storm ripped through Folkshore. No one was harmed, but Folkshore station has been damaged.'

Damaged! How am I going to get home now?

'We've already had word that local businessman and philanthropist, Rumpelstiltskin Gold, who regularly consults with the Assembly, has pledged to help cover the cost of the damage to the station. Let's hope this is not another scheme by the Assembly after their disastrous regeneration plans.'

I need to get out of here fast. Ignoring my growing head-ache, I weave through people and jog down the stairs. Red said she was going to help me. If I can't get out through the station, there must be another way out. There *has* to be.

As I leave Greenwood, the dry heat hits me and I'm sweating in seconds. Yesterday there was a storm and now a heatwave. What's wrong with this place?

The scorching sun is so low that it's basically perched on my shoulder, breathing its hot breath down my neck. Pulling off my coat, I battle the heat and trek back the same way I came yesterday. The pastel cottages are even more striking in the light. Searching for my camera, I rest my shoulder on the corner of the first house and lift the camera to my eye. I adjust the lens a few times, checking to make sure I have the right shot of the narrowing road, before I take a few photos.

The familiar tickle travels up my throat.

'Achoo! Achoo!' Am I allergic to something in Folkshore?

On the high street, the trees provide minimal shade. The street is packed with humans and animals. The frog conductor from yesterday was nothing compared to all this. Foxes, cats, dogs and other animals walk around like humans. How is this normal? Bisi asked my parents for a dog when we were younger. My parents asked her, 'Do you have dog money to pay for it?' We took that as a no.

Stocky pink pigs stuffed into police uniforms are stationed at various points on the long street, their beady eyes tracking and their snouts sniffing for a hint of trouble. Was this what Ty and Sebastian were chatting about? The police are literally pigs here.

A piece of paper brushes against my Converses, and I catch it before it blows away.

MISSING PERSON
Esmerelda Rubio
32 years old, Spanish, medium brown hair, brown eyes, birthmark on her neck. Last seen January 4th, 2023, wearing black jeans and a green turtleneck. If you have seen Esmeralda or know of her whereabouts, please contact us.

This was a few months ago. In the picture, Esmerelda is standing in front of a shop on the high street, which is now covered in scaffolding and plastic sheets.

A short, mixed-race woman with brown skin and the curliest hair stands outside a bakery, her hands on her hips, glaring at the police pigs. She squints, shielding her eyes from the sun as white powder blows off her forehead.

'You have something here...' I say, pointing to her head.

Using her sleeve, the woman scrubs at her forehead. 'Thank you, honey. I'm such a klutz. I'm always getting flour everywhere but in the bowl.'

She can probably tell I'm not from here from the lost look in my eyes. When we first visited Nigeria, they could smell that we were 'from abroad'.

'Do you need something?' she asks.

I *do* need something. I need to know how to get out of this strange place with the weird luminous trees, storms and talking animals.

'Do you know where the library is, please?' I ask.

She pauses for a second and smiles like I've told a joke. 'Which library are you after? There are around five libraries in this part of Folkshore.'

I try to remember if Red told me which library she'd be at, but I come up with nothing.

'Hmm, are you looking for a specific book? Maybe that'll help me narrow it down. I know Folkshore like the back of my hand.'

'I'm looking for Red. I don't know if you know her.'

'Red Riding Hood with the red pixie cut?' she asks.

Red Riding Hood?

She nudges my shoulder, playfully. 'Of course I know *that* Red. *Everyone* knows Red. I'm friends with her grandma. Why didn't you just say that?'

Because I didn't know you knew her.

'If you continue down the high street, you'll see the library Red works at. My name is Cinderella, by the way, but everyone calls me Cindy.'

They've got the fairy tales all wrong. Since when was Cinderella mixed race, Red Riding Hood Jamaican and Prince Charming Irish? Also, Rapunzel *definitely* looks Nigerian.

'I didn't catch your name, sweetie.'

Because I didn't give it. If my mum knew I was about to lie again, I would be her main prayer point at church, but the police pigs might be after me, so she'll understand.

Who am I kidding? She won't.

'Leah... I'm... er... Red's cousin.'

'Why didn't you say that? Any cousin of Red's is family to me.' She steps back towards the bakery's entrance. 'The breakfast crowd will be in soon. Stop by Pumpkin Time anytime and I'll fix you up with something sweet.' Cindy offers a smile as sweet as her words before disappearing into her bakery. My belly wants me to follow her, but my mind is made up. I need to get out of here.

As I march down the road towards the library, the trees beside me pulse. As I move closer, I hear shallow breathing.

'Urghh.'

I stumble into the road. A group of cyclists come flying out of nowhere, but they're not *normal* cyclists because this place isn't normal. They're giraffes, cycling in bright tracksuits, their tall necks bent over the handles.

'Watch it!' one of them shouts.

They whizz past, disorientating me further. I stagger back onto the pavement. Is it my heart thumping, or the trees?

Like the rest of Folkshore, the library is a cottage-style building made of turquoise stone with a dark teal steeple at the top. It reminds me of St Joseph's, where the only thing I had to worry about was exams.

The AC hits my sweaty face as I step through the automatic doors, and I'm in heaven. Red leans over a textbook in the corner of the library, but looks up after hearing the patter of my Converses on the lino floor.

'Hey, cuz!' she calls and bursts out laughing.

'It's not even funny! I can't believe you told Mal that I was your cousin.'

Red waves her hand dismissively. 'What were we supposed to tell her? That we snuck into main London, and you came back with us? If my gran knew what I was doing, she would knock me upside my head. The police in Folkshore don't play around. We have to be careful.'

My stomach quivers at the mention of the police. 'I heard they're looking for someone who came into Folkshore last night.'

She eyes me. 'Yeah, I heard that too.'

'Did you watch the news?' I ask. 'How am I gonna get back now that the station is destroyed? And I can't even call home because of the silly restrictions.'

Red shrugs. 'I dunno yet, but don't worry because it won't even feel like you're gone to your family.'

'What do you mean?'

She sighs deeply, as if I just asked her to carry all the library books on her head. 'Folkshore runs on a different time to main London. Folkshore Standard Time.'

Where have I heard that before?

The Chronicles of Folkshore. At approximately 7.45 Folkshore Standard Time, an unidentified person enters Folkshore...

'It feels like weeks here, but not a lot of time will have passed there,' Red explains. 'It depends on how long you stay. It's a Folkshore thing.'

I scoff. 'I've had enough of this place. I bet the storm and the heatwave are Folkshore things too.'

'No, they're not.' Red shakes her head. 'All the weather changes happened *after* the Reckoning.'

'What is this Reckoning you keep talking about?' I ask. 'You know what? I don't even care. Please can you just help me get back home?'

'I said I would help you, didn't I?' Red rolls her eyes at me. 'And anyways, you can't tell *anyone* that you came into

Folkshore. I'm not having the pigs after us. You know what, I'll take you to my grandma. She knows everything about Folkshore. If there's another way to get out, she'll know it.'

My head throbs and I feel like I'm going to be sick. 'Why can't *you* just help me? You guys managed to sneak out—'

Red slams her book shut and whispers, 'Why are you talking so loudly? We weren't supposed to know about the tunnel or sneak out. Remember those restrictions I was telling you about?'

'Yeah?'

'We're supposed to have ID cards and get permission to leave Folkshore, but we didn't want to get into all that, so we found another way out.'

The fake ticket makes sense now. But why would they need permission to leave?

'How is your grandma gonna help me then? Isn't there another tunnel I can take somewhere?'

In fairy tales, don't they have magical portals? If they want me to start shouting abracadabra, I'll do it.

Red points an acrylic nail at me. 'You ask too many damn questions. My grandma has lived in Folkshore forever. Trust me, she'll know something.'

'And the tunnels?'

What is she not telling me?

'It was Princey who told us about that tunnel, alright,' she breathes. 'I don't know nothing else. If you see him, you can ask him yourself, but don't mention my name.'

'Alright, I won't say nothing, but can we go and see your grandma now? I need to get back home.'

'You're lucky I've finished my holiday revision already. I'll take you now.'

Chapter 6

As we walk back towards the high street, music streams through Red's headphones. She sings along to a song I recognise. *How can someone with such a bad voice have so much confidence?*

She breaks out into a choreographed dance with her elbows sticking out and a whine added in.

'You listen to Stella B?'

Red stops dancing and grins. 'Yeah, *everyone* knows who she is. Just because Folkshore isn't the main part of London doesn't mean we don't have taste.'

'Well, the London *I* know doesn't have talking animals, and why do you guys all have fairy-tale names? Is your name really Red Riding Hood?'

'Yeah, but don't call me that,' she warns me. 'It's Red to you. My family call me Destiny. The fairy-tale names are just how things are here. They've always been like that.'

Red pauses outside a shop painted yellow and black with a sign at the top: *Giselle's Hair and Beauty Palace.*

'Why are we stopping here?' I ask, trying not to sound too annoyed. 'I thought we were going to talk to your grandma.'

'I know, but I'll be quick. I promise.'

She doesn't give me a chance to say anything before she pushes the door open and goes inside.

Giselle's Hair and Beauty Palace is well lit with individual styling stations and floor-to-ceiling mirrors. The soft bass in the background creates a chilled vibe as women chat while getting their hair and nails done.

Everyone calls out to Red.

'Hey, Red!'

'How you doing, beautiful?'

'Hey, family,' Red replies and waves. 'Cuz. Have you got any food? I'm starving.'

She strolls up to a tall woman with long black locs. They kind of look alike.

'Yuh nuh hav mannaz?' The woman kisses her teeth, ignoring Red as she sews a track of Brazilian hair onto a customer's cornrows. 'No "hello Giselle." No "how you doing, Giselle?"'

Some of the customers laugh at this. Red tries to hug her cousin, but she's not having it and steps out of the way. 'You know I love you, Giselle.'

Giselle stares at her for a second then motions to the back of the shop with her head. 'Go and look in the container at the bottom of the fridge.'

Red squeals, hugging her before sprinting to the back of the salon.

'You need to stop moving your head,' Giselle mutters to the client sitting in the chair before speaking to me. 'You can sit over there.' She points to the waiting area in the corner.

Red comes back in, swaying to the music, a small plastic

container in her hands. I can tell what it is just from the smell. Curry goat with white rice. I'm so hungry, man.

Red plonks herself beside me, tearing into the tender goat meat with her fork.

'Thanks for yesterday, Giselle,' Red says, her mouth full. 'Mal really thought that you were Leah's mum.'

Giselle clears her throat and puts on a call centre voice. 'Yes, this is Leah's mother speaking. Yes, that girl doesn't listen at all. She wanted to see her cousin, but she doesn't get on with her grandma. I just wanted her somewhere safe.'

They burst out laughing. Red continues eating like I'm not sitting here waiting for her.

'Be honest with me, Destiny. Where did you really go yesterday?' Giselle asks, moving over to the sink with dirty combs in her hand. 'I don't want you to get in any trouble.'

Red drops the fork back into the container. 'We made sure no one saw us.'

Shaking her head, Giselle switches off the running water. 'You keep on chatting about "we" this and "us" that. Who am I talking to now? Mi nuh bizniz 'bout nuh body else but you, Destiny.' Giselle moves back to the client, picking up the Brazilian track she left on the side, and begins sewing. 'Keep your head down and don't get into trouble with that good-for-nothing boyfriend of yours. I thought you wanted to be a lawyer. You need to keep focused. If your parents come back here and see what you're doing, you know they won't be impressed.'

Giselle sounds like my parents when they tell me to keep

focused on school. They don't want anything to distract me, so I stopped asking them to let me go anywhere. Everything but studying is a distraction to them. The one time I asked my dad if I could go to the gym with Priya, he said I should 'exercise my books'.

Red's gaze flicks upwards before settling on Giselle again. 'It's not even Ty's fault—he wasn't even there. And I still want to be a lawyer.'

'That's what I thought,' Giselle replies, ending the conversation.

Red throws the container in the bin and leaves Giselle's salon, me trailing behind. The trek to the main junction is quiet. I don't know Red well, but I know her silence isn't normal.

'I get it,' I say quietly. 'The pressure from family.'

'I don't wanna talk about it.'

If she doesn't want to talk about it, then I won't. By Goblin Grove, we pass sleek black apartment buildings with curved windows and balconies. They stand out against the other buildings in Folkshore. They don't fit in here.

Down the alleyway, the graffiti on the walls moves alongside us, telling a story. Of course, the art is alive here. A young girl in a bright orange jacket wanders along the wisteria brick with her hair flapping around her. Unknown to her, a thick gloomy human-shaped shadow follows her and she doesn't see it until it's too late. A ghostly hand surges out of the shadow, puncturing the girl's chest, and she leaks white light, like the kind in the lamppost.

'My grandma used to tell me these stories about Shriekers when I was younger.' Red points to the dark shadow.

'Prince was joking about them yesterday. What are they?'

'According to my grandma, Shriekers are these evil creatures who eat rude children.'

I laugh at that. '*Just* rude children? No one else?'

'Exactly. I know she only told me so I wouldn't act bad,' Red replies. 'We're here.'

The community centre is unlike any other building I've seen before. Similar to the station, it's made of glass, but the glass has a sandy texture and the shimmering roof sits on top like a plane ready to take off. As we get closer, the sun reflects off it, creating a rainbow-like effect.

Inside, Rapunzel and Westley stand in front of a group of people, holding up a pile of missing persons flyers. They're wearing matching all-black outfits.

'The Assembly are using this regeneration as a distraction. They think we'll ignore what's really going on, but we won't,' Rapunzel barks. 'Not when our people are missing.'

'Who's missing?' I whisper to Red, pausing.

'People in Folkshore. You see them one day and then they're gone. Last week it was Jack and the week before, it was Aurora. Giselle was supposed to do her hair.'

The flyer on the street. 'Why though? People can't just *go* missing.'

'No one knows why—that's why Rap and Westley are getting people to look for clues around Folkshore.'

Calmly, Westley steps forward to address the group of

teens, which includes Ty and Prince and some other people from Greenwood. 'We're going out there today to spread the word and raise awareness about what's happening.'

A young girl around seven hangs around Rap like Bisi used to do with me. This was many years ago when Bisi didn't find everything I do annoying. Rap fishes her phone out of her pocket and hands it over to the girl.

'My grandma's over there,' Red says, pulling my attention away.

Red strolls to the other side of the room, then bends down to hug a petite black woman with curly grey hair pulled up into a tight, neat bun.

'Did you miss me, Gran?' Red asks. 'Hey, Auntie Pauline.' She waves at a black woman around my mum's age.

'Miss you?' Red's grandma cuts her eyes. 'Why would I miss you? I see you every day. You're always eating up my food.'

Auntie Pauline chuckles. 'How are you, m'dear?'

'I'm blessed—can't complain,' Red replies. 'Gran, this is my friend, Leah. She's doing a project on Folkshore.'

I stop my mouth from falling open at the lies spewing from Red's mouth.

'You can tell her more about Folkshore because you know everything about it.'

'Of course I can,' Red's grandma agrees, 'but go and make me a cup of tea first, and make sure the water is hot.'

But instead of going straight to the kitchen, she stops off and talks to Rap.

Red's gran places a domino down and pats the empty chair beside her. 'Come and sit down, child. I'm Patsy. What do you want to know about Folkshore?'

I sit down. 'You've been in Folkshore for long, right?'

'I've been here for almost 50 years. I raised two children and four grandchildren here, but I didn't always live in Folkshore. When I was young, I came to London from Jamaica with Gerald, my husband.' She smiles fondly, lost in her own thoughts. 'My friend, Eustace, kept on telling me to come and live here. Folkshore wasn't common knowledge; it was only through word of mouth that you heard about it. I went to a special ticket office in London and put Eustace's name down on a form because he referred me. They handed me this purple one-way ticket to Folkshore. I had to wait for a particular train at my station. Folkshore has been such a *wonderful* place.'

Auntie Pauline slams a domino down on the table. 'Until that Reckoning. The Assembly restrict us now, like we're criminals. We can't move properly. We can't speak to who we want without telling them. I bet they also want to know what I ate for breakfast.'

I want to ask more about the Assembly, but if I'm a Folkshorian, I should know who they are already.

'And now Folkshore station has been destroyed,' Auntie Pauline says.

'Isn't there any other way out of Folkshore?' I ask.

'Not that I know of,' Grandma Pat replies.

Chapter 7

I wake up with the worst headache ever, my sweat-drenched top clinging to my chest. I try to forget the dream, but I can't. I heard those words over and over again.

The Chronicles of Folkshore. At approximately 7.45 Folkshore Standard Time, an unidentified person enters Folkshore...

Folkshore was falling apart. I don't need a dream to tell me this place is a mess. Our government might be suspect, but this place is something else. How can they stop people from leaving? What really happened during the Reckoning? No one seems to want to tell me anything. And why are the police *still* looking for someone who came into Folkshore?

I pick up my phone. There's still no signal. My finger hits the photo icon instead and I scroll back through memories, like Pree and me on a school trip to Spain. She spent the whole train journey cussing Brad for something dumb he'd said. I laugh. I get to the photo of where we'd surprised Mum with a party for her birthday and she transformed into some Nollywood actress with her fake screams, even though she had told us the week before which outfit she wanted for the surprise party.

Scrolling through hundreds of pictures, I pause at one in particular, and the smile is snatched off my face as quickly as it came. The picture is of Deji and me standing in a ball pit. I remember it—it was a week before Deji went to the hospital for tests because he hadn't been feeling well. Everyone thought it was a cold or something, because Deji was *never* sick. I hope he's okay. God, send me some kind of sign.

Knock. Knock.

I make sure there's no sleep in my eyes before I shout. 'Come in!'

Branna appears in an all-white two-piece trouser set with her dark, wavy hair loose. Could Branna be a sign?

'Rise and shine, babes!' she shouts. 'Mal wants to speak to you. Why are you lookin' at me like that?' She stares down. 'Is my tit hanging out or something?'

'Nah, forget it.'

Bran's phone pings five times in a row, but she ignores it. 'It's just Harvey,' she explains. 'You know how it is. If you let 'em, they'll take the absolute piss out of you.'

I nod. 'Yeah, I know.'

I don't know what she's talking about. I'm not saying I don't chat to boys, but maths is my boyfriend, and he keeps me warm at night with all his decimals.

'Ty said you're from North Folkshore,' Bran comments.

I didn't even know there *was* a North Folkshore.

'I used to live up in main London, but I fell out with my mum. Someone said that's why you're here too.'

Falling out with my mum would equal a one-way ticket to Nigeria. She doesn't want 'wayward children'.

'I needed somewhere to stay so I came to Folkie, but that was before the Reckoning cos they wouldn't have allowed me in afterwards,' Bran continues.

'I was away from... er... Folkshore when the Reckoning happened,' I lie. 'I don't know a lot of the details. What happened?'

Gregg always told us that we should find the story, and there's *definitely* a story here.

'Long story short. There was this bloke that was killed from the Assembly,' Bran explains, but that only leaves me more confused. 'Sorry, I don't even know all the details myself.'

Maybe if I knew more about this Reckoning, I can figure out a way to get home. 'If I wanted to find out more about what happened, where can I go?'

Bran opens my door. 'Pascal can help you. He owns the library off the high street. I know him, so I can introduce you. Laters. Gary's been on hold for 20 minutes.'

Gary? I thought it was Harvey.

After climbing the first flight of stairs to Mal's office, I'm out of breath; this is what I get for just 'exercising my books'.

'What's the craic?' Prince asks, blocking my way.

He's wearing another black hoodie with a grey T-shirt of a band I've never heard of. What is he doing here? I didn't know he lived here too.

'I'm greetin' you.' He chuckles and then teases. 'All you uncultured folk.'

'I'm cultured.' I point to myself. 'Who is the "you" you're chatting about? I know you can't greet me in Yoruba.'

'Give me a shot.' He crosses his arms.

Prince really thinks he's *that* guy. 'Alright. Say "e káàárò." It means good morning.'

Prince cracks his bony knuckles and extends his neck as if he's about to do something special. 'Karoo.'

I snicker and step past him.

'Give me another go!' Prince shouts from behind me.

Leaving him on the stairs, I climb up and pause outside Mal's office. I still can't believe her name is Maleficent.

'Yes?' Mal calls from inside.

How did she know I was standing here?

Twisting the handle, I stick my head through the door.

'I thought it was you,' Mal says, looking up from her work. 'Sorry we haven't had a chance to talk properly. It's been crazy around here—or more crazy than usual, anyways.' She gestures to the chair in front of her desk. 'I'm not sure how much Red has told you about Greenwood but let me properly introduce myself again. I am Maleficent Campbell, and I'm the director of the Folkshore branch of Greenwood. We help young people get back on their feet. For other folk, it's just a place to stay if they don't have family here. We have branches in other hidden places like in Whitemount, which my friend Alice Everbee helps run.'

There are *other* hidden places? I can't keep up!

'Yes, there are other hidden places, like Folkshore, in major cities around the world.' Mal studies me from across the table, not breaking eye contact. 'But you should know that already.'

I stumble over my words. 'Yeah, of course... erm... I know that. I'm from here.'

Mal ignores my slip up and describes what else they do at Greenwood before sliding a form over to me. 'I should've given you this on the first night, but it was pretty late. It's nothing official, but we need to keep a record of all the young people who stay here.'

I look down at the form. It's asking for my full name, my Folkshore address, and other things I have no clue about.

I fiddle with the pen.

Softening her tone, Mal says, 'I completely understand, Leah. I don't want to make you feel uncomfortable. Why don't you fill out the form and bring it back to me? Sound good?'

'Thanks. I'll bring it back.'

I'll bring it back after Red fills out this form of lies. I take the form and stand up from the chair, but Mal remembers something else.

'My friend Cinderella. You might know her? Cinderella Asamoah, who owns the Pumpkin Time bakery?'

The perky woman with flour on her forehead.

'She's short on staff at the moment, and I know most secondary schools are on holiday so it would give you something to do before school starts again. Cindy could use some help from a smart, capable young woman such as yourself.'

How about I help myself out of this place?

Mal seems to sense my hesitation. 'It would keep you busy—and it's a *paid* position.'

Now why didn't she start with that? Do they pay in pounds here or fairy dust, though?

If I work with Cinderella, I could get some answers about Folkshore and how to get out of here.

'I can help Cinderella out.'

'Perfect. Thanks, Leah. I owe you one. You can stop by there today.'

Library first, then Cindy's.

Our conversation ends when Mal's phone rings. Grabbing my bag, I leave her office and head towards the doors, bumping into someone coming into Greenwood.

'Sorry, excuse me.' The same hypnotic golden eyes I saw in a photo on the wall are peering down at me with interest.

Rumpelstiltskin Gold.

'Are you a new resident at Greenwood?' he asks. 'I don't believe I've seen you here before.'

'Yeah, um, I'm not *really* new. My cousin lives here. Not here, here, but she lives close. My cousin is Red. I'm not getting on with my family right now so I'm staying here for a little bit.'

Smooth, Fola.

'I know exactly what you mean about difficulties with family because I've had my fair share. Well, I hope you find Greenwood most accommodating.'

The back of my neck itches as the stress of the situation builds. 'Thank you,' I respond and move out of the way so that Rumpelstiltskin can enter the building, leaving me and my lying self behind.

I shiver as the sky darkens and the clouds cluster together, creating an ominous silhouette over Folkshore. Torrential rain pours down. After a few seconds, my clothes are drenched.

A ball of hail smashes by my foot. A second later, another one strikes my arm. It feels like I've been shot. Dodging the hail attack, I run down the flooded high street, water seeping into my trainers.

Folkshorians rush or trot about with newspapers over their heads, while others drag in displays and find shelter. The towering trees have turned into themselves to shield from the hail.

I run towards the steeple of the library as if it's a lifeline. A badger dressed in green corduroy trousers and a button-up shirt meets me at the entrance with a box of tissues. 'Oh, dearie me, the weather is *particularly* dreadful today.'

'There you are, Leah!' Bran shouts from inside the library.

I scramble to get away from the badger's beady eyes. I

feel bad, but it's only been two days and it's all still too weird for me.

'Is your friend alright?' the badger whispers from behind his paw.

Bran looks at him and then back to me before cackling. 'She's scared of you, Pascal. It was the same for me when I first came here. I was like, what the actual fuck?'

I flinch.

'What? You don't like swearing?' Bran asks with a smile on her face. 'I tried a swear jar once, but I fucking ballsed that up. I mean, I *messed* it up. Anyways, Pascal is a Folkshorian. It's part of what Folkie is. Shouldn't you be used to it?'

She's right. Leah would be used to it.

I plaster a smile on my face, even though Pascal is scaring me. 'Um, yeah. I'm cool with it. Where I live in Folkshore has... erm... more humans.'

The black fur above Pascal's mouth rises to reveal his incisors and canines.

God, I can't.

Bran pulls herself up onto the main helpdesk to sit. 'Pascal, how's Jackie?'

'Jackie is great, thank you,' Pascal replies, flashing more of his teeth. 'She has a new stew dish for you to try. Can you get down from the desk, please? I've told you many times that it's not an appropriate place to sit.'

Bran pops her gum and jumps down to the floor, sending drops of water everywhere.

Pascal wheezes and covers his mouth with his paws. 'Oh, excuse me.'

'You sure you're okay, Pas?' Bran asks, biting her lip. 'You've had that cough for ages.'

'Yes, yes, I am perfectly fine, Branna,' Pascal replies. 'You don't need to worry about me. It's just a little cough—and remember, I always feel rather run down at this time of the year. What can I help you with?' he asks me. 'I'm sure you didn't come here to hear me prattle on.'

'The Reckoning,' I start. 'I want to do some research on it.'

'Such a tragic moment in Folkshore's history. You can find all you need over on those pink shelves,' Pascal directs, pointing to the other end of the library. 'It will be listed under R.'

'Thanks, Pascal.'

I didn't get a chance to look at the library properly yesterday. Paintings of Folkshore and Folkshorians cover the turquoise ceiling.

I locate the folder marked 'Reckoning' right at the corner of the pink shelf. Using the rolling ladder, I climb up, balancing on my right leg to reach the thick folder.

'Did you find it?' Bran's voice startles me, making me wobble. 'Easy!'

'You can't sneak up on people like that!' I shout, clutching my chest.

Bran sits on the table behind me. 'Sorry, mate. I thought you heard me coming.'

Ignoring her, I reach up, slowly, to get the folder, then step off the ladder. I move to the other end of the long table and open the folder, which is filled to the brim with articles.

'Are you searching for clues?' Bran asks. 'I can help you. We can be like Sherlock Holmes and Wottie!'

I laugh for a minute. 'You mean Watson.'

Bran shrugs, a cheeky grin on her face. 'It's all elementary, babes.'

A folded piece of paper is lodged in the base of the binder. It's an article written by Anna Tsang a year ago.

'This day will forever be known as the Reckoning,' I read. *'Jack Crombie was arrested for murdering Assembly member Duke Everbee, and for attempting to expose Folkshore to the outside world. Rumpelstiltskin Gold, a local businessman, testified against his former business partner, Jack. The Assembly have since put in restrictions to protect Folkshore.'*

Restrictions like making people have an ID card to travel, and monitoring people's calls.

'After the Reckoning, that's when Folkie's weather changed,' Bran says. 'Folkie was proper nice before. It was *way* better than staying with Mum. Now it looks like the fur balls that my nan's cat used to cough up.'

After reading other articles and accounts of the Reckoning, I close the folder and put it back on the shelf. Now I know what happened, but I'm no closer to finding a way back.

I could ask Prince about the tunnels, but will he help me? I'm not even supposed to know that he knows.

'Did you find what you were looking for?' Pascal asks.

'Kinda,' I reply. 'Thanks for helping.'

As I'm about to leave, something pops back into my head from the nightmare I had. 'This might sound weird, but do you know what the chronicles of Folkshore is? Is it a book?' I ask, the questions tumbling out.

Pascal's eyes widen. '*The Chronicles of Folkshore* is a book. I know of the many rumours linked to it. Some people believe it exists; others don't, but I do. It's very powerful as it takes on many forms: it might appear as a scroll, a book, or something else entirely. The book is supposed to document all of Folkshore's history. It's special indeed.'

'How is it special?'

Pascal leans closer and whispers, 'Apparently it holds the secrets to Folkshore. They say that *The Chronicles of Folkshore* can get you wherever you want to go.'

'Wherever you want to go,' I whisper back. 'What does that even mean?'

Chapter 8

My gaze roams over the cakes on display in the window of the Pumpkin Time bakery. From the round carrot cake to the towering chocolate cake with icing dripping down the side like teardrops, Cindy's desserts are the best I've seen in a long time.

As I push open the door to the bakery, a loud ring resounds, drawing Cindy's attention to the door. The bakery is spacious. While the walls are painted canary yellow, the wooden furniture is white, including the circular tables and beech chairs.

Cindy's yellow crocs squeak as she comes towards me. 'Thanks so much for offering to help me at such short notice, Leah. I still have some cupcakes to make for tomorrow *and* I got a last-minute surprise birthday order from one of my repeat customers,' she says, speeding through her words. 'It's her daughter's fifth tomorrow and she wants a cartoon cake. "No princesses," she told me. Why don't you wash your hands and grab an apron? There are little hair nets in the corner too.'

Can you get whiplash from how fast someone is talking?

Groaning, Cindy plants her head in her hands. 'I'm sorry. I'm doing it again, aren't I? My daughters are constantly telling me that I talk too quickly. Let's go into the back so I can show you what's what before I scare you away for good. Have you made cupcakes before?' she asks.

'Nope, but I've eaten them. Does that count?'

'Of course.' Cindy beams. 'What are cupcakes really without tasters?'

I like how she thinks.

She pushes a laminated recipe card and two bowls towards me. 'Here you go.'

I measure out the dry ingredients for the red velvet cupcakes, add them and whisk. Then in a second bowl, I whisk the remaining ingredients together before combining everything. Carefully, I scoop the batter into cupcake tins and put the tray in the oven. After 20 minutes, I take my babies out of the oven, and almost shed a tear to see them so grown and soft.

'You're a natural,' Cindy praises me. 'We'll let the cupcakes cool before we start icing them.'

Cinderella brings us a few slices of red velvet cake and Earl Grey tea in a teapot with the label dangling down the side. The sweet cake invades my mouth and crumbles on my tongue. Leave Folkshore? Who said that?

'Thanks again for coming today. I had some help before, but she up and left. I guess it's pretty standard, all things considered.'

I blow on the tea, taking a small sip which burns my tongue. 'What do you mean?'

'You probably already know of this, but with the Assembly's regeneration plans, people are taking the money offered for their businesses and leaving Folkshore. Leonard, for example. He was one of the people who helped me get this bakery.' Cindy stares off into the distance. 'He used to own the antique shop opposite me, but six months ago he vanished. The Assembly rep said he took the money offered to him and left Folkshore, but why wouldn't he say goodbye?' She looks back at me. 'It doesn't feel right at all.'

The antique shop across the road is covered in plastic sheets and scaffolding. Are they doing construction everywhere?

'What are they changing it into?' I ask.

'No one knows, and the Assembly won't tell anyone. It's not right. With all these people missing, I think that's what we should be worrying about, instead of regeneration plans.'

Can no one see how weird this all is? It sounds like the plot to at least five different crime shows. How can people be going missing, and Folkshore's council isn't doing anything about it?

Cindy sighs. 'Soon it won't feel like Folkshore anymore. I'm glad I still have this place.'

'Your bakery is so nice,' I reply, looking around. 'I see pictures of places like this online all the time.'

'Thanks for the compliment. Do you mean online some-where like Flashgram?'

'Flash what?' I ask, confused.

'Flashgram.' Cindy rubs at her forehead with a frown. 'It's pretty popular. I'm surprised you don't know it. You can post all your pictures and videos there for people to like.'

'Yeah, er, yeah, Flashgram,' I reply, stumbling over my words. 'I forget sometimes.'

'Honestly, I can't keep up with all these new social media trends either,' Cindy agrees, which stops me from freaking out. 'It's definitely not easy starting your own business, but I had a great support system behind me.'

'Support from your family?'

'Yes, especially my late husband, Michael,' she says softly, stroking her ring finger. 'He would've loved to see all of this, but not so much everything else.' Cindy clears our plates and mugs away. 'Okay, let's get to icing the rest of the cakes before my girls get back from their music lesson with my sister.'

I follow her into the back, and Cindy shows me how to use one of those piping things you see on TV to create some icing swirls on the cake.

'Cinderella, do you have a Flashgram account for your business?'

She looks up from wiping the table. 'Cindy. Call me Cindy, and no, I don't have one set up, but my daughter, Maya, talks about it all the time. Why?'

'Because your cakes are beautiful. I think it would be good for your business. People can like and share your photos, and you can get more customers. I can try and set one up for you now if you want.'

I hope it's easy to set up or I'll look stupid.

'But won't I need professional photos?'

I walk back to get my camera from my bag and dangle it in front of her. 'I'll take some.'

I lift the camera up to my right eye and take a few practice shots for Cindy to see. The light is great—there's natural light pouring in through the windows.

'Oh, that one looks amazing,' she says, looking at the pictures. 'You're really good at this. So, what happens next?'

'We make you a Flashgram. We can do it now?'

'Oh, yes please.'

Thankfully, it's pretty easy to set up an account for her. In ten minutes, she's already got pictures and some likes.

Cindy smiles and touches my arm. 'People are liking the pictures! This is great, thank you.'

My response is cut short by the ding of the bakery door.

'Mum, guess what happened to me today,' a young girl, who has Cindy's complexion and eyes, says. As she runs over to Cindy, the beads at the end of her cornrows clack together. She hoists herself up into one of the high stools.

Cindy snorts.

'Hey, sis.' Cinderella's older sister, I'm guessing, walks in with a smaller brown-haired girl a few seconds later. 'Who's this?'

All eyes focus on me and I wave, awkwardly. 'Hi.'

'This is Leah, and she's been helping today,' Cindy explains. 'She's a lifesaver.'

Cindy points at the woman first, then at the girl on the

stool, then at the younger, quieter girl, who is staring at me. 'This is my big sister Anastasia, my oldest daughter and chatterbox Maya, and my youngest, Danielle or Dani.'

Every time Cindy calls me Leah, I want to say something, but I can't tell her the truth, especially with the police sniffing around. I don't know who I can trust.

Anastasia offers me a big smile like Cindy's. 'It's nice to meet you, Leah. Thanks so much for helping my Cindy out.'

A family of smilers. Dani stops in front of me and flashes a shy smile as Maya helps her up onto one of the high stools.

Anastasia tugs Cindy on the arm, drawing her away from us, but we can hear everything. 'Please just try and talk to him. He really wants to see you and the kids.'

'For just one day, I don't want to talk about him. Please.'

I wonder who they're talking about.

'If something happens...' Anastasia starts, but the look on Cindy's face stops her. 'Okay, I've heard you.'

Anastasia moves in front of Cindy and smooths down her hair. 'You'll never stop being my little sis, no matter how stubborn you are.'

Maya's face appears over my shoulder. 'What you got there?'

I lower my camera and show her the pictures I took.

'Oh, that one's *perfect*. The lighting is everything.'

I love her already.

'It's for your mum's Flashgram,' I reply.

Maya starts laughing and shakes her head. '*My* mum has Flash. Gram. Not possible.'

'Yeah, look. I set it up for her.'

Maya uses her hand to punctuate each word. 'I've been telling my mum since *forever* that Flashgram is where it's at.'

'Telling me what?' Cinderella jumps in.

'That I'd be a great social media manager,' Maya replies. 'I can get your followers up.'

Cindy clutches her chest. 'Will it be free since I'm your mother?'

'You'll get a discount on my services because you're family... just £500.'

I laugh.

'Okay, that's enough.' Cindy laughs with me. 'Say goodbye to Leah. Auntie Anastasia is taking you up to the flat now.'

Maya huffs and hops off the stool, while Dani shuffles out after her sister and aunt. Clearing up the rest of the things we used, I start washing up the plates, like I would at home.

Cindy shooes me away. 'You don't have to do that. I'll finish up. Go be young and have fun.'

'Alright, I'll see you later.'

As soon as I step out onto the high street, the cruel chill in the air makes me shudder, and I can barely see through the thick fog. The familiar itching sensation works its way up my throat, and I sneeze into a tissue.

My footsteps echo across the deserted streets. Ever since I've come to this place, it's been one thing after the other. I should've stayed at home and watched YouTube instead. You know what I would've had, huh? I would've had banging eyebrows and healthy, natural hair, but look what I have instead. I can't even feel my toes.

The sensation of tiny insects crawling up my back makes me speed up. The cold air freezes my lungs, giving me a tickly cough. I burrow deeper into my coat.

A shrill shriek cuts through the night, and a vision flickers in my mind. It's too blurry for me to make out anything except a spark of blue electricity in the sky, with bodies lying still on the ground. As quickly as the vision came, it's gone, and I feel empty inside. What was that?

'How's it going?' someone asks, startling me. Prince appears near me, a skateboard tucked under his arm. 'I'm sorry, I didn't mean to scare ya.'

I wait for my racing heart to settle before I respond. 'Why... did you do that?' My voice trembles. 'I'm tired of this place. I'm done. I know about the tunnels. You're going to help me get back home.'

Chapter 9

'It's Day 4 in Folkshore.' I speak to my camera. 'If anyone finds this video, just know that I'm never having fun again. Mum, I'm sorry. Deji, stop laughing, Pree, stop thinking about if this video will go viral. Dad, apparently, I'm *not* smarter than this. Roti, you can have the £20 hidden under my pillow—and Bisi, stop touching my clothes. A storm destroyed Folkshore station and people are going missing, but the Assembly won't do anything about it. I might have someone who can help me.'

Switching off the camera, I slump back onto the bed and throw the pillow across the room in frustration at the situation.

What are you doing, Fola? There's a certain tattooed boy you need to find.

Greenwood is eerily silent as I slip through it like smoke. I find Prince hunched over dozens of textbooks at the kitchen table. He is hoodie-less, which is some sort of miracle. It's almost poetic, the way the tattoos snake up his arm, as if they're in some sort of race. I spot some letters that aren't in English, and wonder what they mean.

'It's Gaelic,' he replies and lifts his head, trapping me with those icy eyes. 'It means you're only as good as your redemption story.'

Did I say that out loud?

'Ya did,' Prince jokes. 'Ya really need to work on that.'

He shoves one textbook away and I see my second love on the page—maths.

It reminds me of something my dad used to say to me. *Be nice to maths and it'll be nice to you.*

'I didn't know that,' Prince says with a crooked smile. 'I'll just take maths out for a date then, shall I?'

Rolling my eyes, I take a seat opposite him. 'But seriously, once you know the method, it's easy.'

Prince releases his low bun from its elastic band and runs his hand through it, straightening out the kinks. 'I don't have a problem with maths. I just have...' he hesitates, 'a lot on my mind.'

I wonder if it has anything to do with what he was in London for, and that phone call at the exhibition.

'My mam is probably rollin' in 'er grave knowing I deferred my exams. I should've taken them last year.'

'I'm not judging you,' I reply, holding my hands up. 'I know what it's like trying to focus on school when there's other stuff going on.'

Deji enters my mind.

'What are you revising?' I ask.

Prince is shaking his head before I even finish talking. 'I got it—don't worry ya head about me.'

So, he's stubborn then.

'Listen, Prince. I'm smart,' I reply simply, even though I haven't been moving smart. 'And I'm great at revising. We can test each other.'

Taking a blank piece of paper, I fold it in half and tear it to create revision cards. I look at the first textbook that catches my eye, and skim-read over information on the First World War. I create revision cards with key terms, timelines and questions to test his memory. I slide them over to Prince, who gawks at the makeshift cards like I'm sliding him something illegal.

'Huh,' he murmurs, scratching his chin.

'And you'll be helping me out too,' I rush to say, because I know I've got him. 'It can be like a study group. I'm revising for my GCSEs as well.'

Prince grips his blond locks as if they're his lifeline, and nods. 'Okay.'

'But only—'

He chuckles. 'I knew it.'

'The tunnels. I *really* need your help to get home,' I reply, the desperation obvious in my voice.

The noise picks up around us as people come into the kitchen. Prince leans forward, lowering his voice so no one but me can hear him. 'And I already told ya yesterday that I can't help ya with that.'

'Prince, I need to find a way out of this place. Please,' I beg.

'What's it to ya?' he asks, leaning back in his chair.

'It's not like I was listening to your conversation at the British Library or anything,' I say, even though I was. 'But it sounds like you need to get back to London too, especially now that the station is destroyed. I'm not supposed to be here. My family is back in London.'

Prince snaps the black hair tie around his wrist a couple times before answering. 'My mate, Chris. He can help ya.'

Ty saunters over in his usual grey tracksuit, a relaxed smile on his face. 'You cool, Leah?'

Prince coughs beside me as I answer to my fake name. 'Yeah, I'm alright.'

'Nice. Let me know if you need anything, yeah? Remember what I said about us being family. If I don't look after you, Red will kill me. Prince, you going to Rap's meeting after the town hall?'

'The Queen will have my head if I miss it,' Prince jokes.

Ty laughs along. 'Yeah, man.' Ty interlocks his fingers and rests them on his face, as if he's deep in thought. 'Rap can be so annoying. If she wasn't Red's best friend, I wouldn't talk to her at all.'

Someone calls to Ty from the other side of the room.

'I'll see you later, Prince.'

If Rap knew Ty was talking about her, that throbbing vein on her head would rupture.

Prince chuckles. 'Bobby. It's what I call that vein on Rap's head.'

'You better not let her hear you saying that.' I laugh along with him. 'What meeting was Ty talking about?'

'It's about the Assembly,' Prince replies, then changes the subject. 'I can take ya to see Chris now. You should bring your camera along too.'

'Yeah,' I reply without thinking. 'Wait. How did you know about my camera?'

'It's been days and that baby's basically attached to ya hands.'

'Don't pretend you know me like that.'

'OK, *Leah*,' he teases.

When we get outside, the weather is stable for once. There's no storm or heatwave but a gentle breeze. At the junction, we turn onto Dragon's Place and head into a part of Folkshore I've never seen before called Enchanted Square. A canal runs along the middle of the street and an enormous, towering tree with a thick trunk sits at the beginning of the street. It has luminous twisty twigs like sparks of electricity, but it's slightly different from the other trees because its pulsating leaves have a white glow to them.

'This is the Hometree,' Prince states. 'Legend says that it was the first tree to grow in Folkshore and all the trees are linked to it. It's the centre of Folkshore.'

'Why do some of the trees glow like the Hometree and others don't?'

Prince shrugs. 'Hell if I know. They all used to glow, but, one by one, they've started to lose their light.'

A man in a Folkshore maintenance shirt stands by the Hometree with a tiny notebook. Kneeling by an out-of-order water hydrant, he checks the yellow device wedged into the

Hometree's soil and notes down his readings. The maintenance man opens a small hatch with other supplies inside and puts his notebook in.

Enchanted Square is full of statues, like one of Rapunzel from the fairy tale, but she's Black and she's cutting off her hair. Underneath each statue is a plaque explaining the history behind it.

Turning down a tight side road, we soon emerge onto Villain's Lane and pause by a wire fence with a gaping hole in it.

'After you.' Prince waits for me to climb through the hole, then follows.

'This,' Prince says, and gestures like a magician revealing his final trick, 'is the Undercroft.'

The Undercroft has high ramps and a massive dip in the centre where skaters spin in the air and land. Bikers chill out on the outskirts, talking. I crouch down with my camera tilted upwards. A skater takes off from the ramp and I capture everything, telling a story through the shots.

It feels separate to Folkshore—like its own world. White pillars around the pit in the centre are covered in the same moving graffiti I saw on the way to the community centre.

We move deeper underground. Spray cans litter the floor as masked artists graffiti the walls. One piece of moving art shows a tiny man creeping. He stops and looks around before taking out a huge can of spray paint. Struggling with the can, he tags 'Undercroft' on one of the walls, and the artwork repeats itself.

A curvy black girl with thick Bantu knots, dressed in black dungarees and dirty white Vans, winks at me. 'Why are you slumming it with him?'

Prince chuckles. 'Cheers, Mia.'

'Well, if it isn't Prince himself,' remarks a short, lean boy around my age with the sides of his blonde hair shaved and a longer section of hair in the middle.

'In the flesh,' Prince replies.

'My name's Chris,' he says to me. 'What's your name, beautiful?'

I roll my eyes. Priya would *love* him.

'Just a little fun. All harmless.' Chris points to my camera. 'What do you shoot?'

'Candids. Short films. Anything, really. What do you do?'

'I respect that,' Chris replies. 'I grace these losers here with my presence, but I'm a computer man.' He whispers to me. 'You need anything hacked, let me know.'

'I brought her here to see you, actually.'

Chris wiggles his bushy eyebrows, which makes me laugh. Prince pushes him back jokingly and uses his body as a barrier. 'Not for that, you tool.' Prince motions for us to move deeper into the tunnels, away from others.

'If this is about that tenner I owe you, Charming, I promise—'

Prince shoves Chris. 'I've told you to stop callin' me that.'

'Tell me about the tunnels,' I state. 'I know I'm not supposed to know, but I need to get back home and Prince said you could help me.'

'Did he now?' Chris says, cocking his head at Prince. 'You have to *promise* this stays between us three. I hear the police have been breathing down people's necks.'

'I promise,' I say.

'I used to work at a retirement home, and I got talking to an old-timer called Eustace. He worked with the Assembly ages ago. Eustace was the one who told me about the tunnels.'

Isn't Eustace Grandma Pat's friend?

Prince asks, 'Watcha thinking?'

'Can I use your phone? I need to call Red.'

Prince passes his phone to me without a word, and I wait until she picks up.

'Hey, Princey.'

'It's me, Leah. You know, your cousin.'

Red laughs. *'What's good, Leah?'*

'This might sound like a mad question, but, if you're at home, can I speak to your grandma?'

'Ermm, why?'

I tug at the collar of my jumper. 'I want to ask her something about what she told me before. It's about Folkshore.'

There's movement at the other end of the phone before Red's grandma answers.

'What can I do for you, dear?'

'Hi, Grandma Pat. I wanted to ask you about your friend Eustace. I think he was the one who told you about Folkshore.'

'Yes, Eustace. What do you want from him?'

'I heard that Eustace used to work for the Assembly, and I wanted to ask him a few questions about it for my project.'

'Ah, yes. It was in the '80s he worked with the Assembly. He used to tell me all kinds of crazy stories. I usually visit him a couple times a month, but I haven't been yet. If it's for school and it's urgent—'

'Yeah, it's really urgent.' Like, 'I could be missing my brother's surgery' urgent and 'my mum could send me to Nigeria' urgent.

'We can go and visit him now. Do you know where the residential home is? You can meet me there, but don't be late.'

'I won't be.'

'He won't like me mentioning this, but it's important you know. Eustace has early-onset dementia which can affect him at times. I believe he can still help you.'

'Thanks for telling me. I'll see you soon.'

Before I get a word out, Prince answers my question. 'Get to Enchanted Square and turn right off Dragon's Place.'

'Thanks, Prince. See you later.'

'Knock, knock,' Grandma Pat says as she pushes Eustace's door open at the end of the corridor in the retirement home.

An older black man with low-cut grey hair and clear eyes is arranging some books on a small wooden shelf.

'Patsy!' Eustace exclaims. 'I'm just looking for that book for you.' He stumbles across the room with his cane, unsteady on his feet.

Grandma Pat shoots across the room, discarding her purse. 'Sit down before you hurt yourself, Eustace.'

Eustace grumbles as she helps him into his seat.

'I'm as strong as I've ever been.' He points to his head. 'You see this brain right here. It's still fresh. Now, introduce me to your young friend. The name's Eustace Banks.'

Resting on his cane, Eustace hoists himself back out of the armchair. Grandma Pat looks like she's ready to cuss him out. He limps towards me and holds out his right hand for me to shake. I grasp it.

'You know what they say about firm handshakes?' he asks, pumping my hand up and down. 'A firm hand means a firm mind.'

'Hi, I'm Leah. I heard you used to work with the Assembly, and I'm doing research for a project. Can I ask you a few questions about it?'

'Patsy, you didn't tell me you were bringing a live one,' Eustace remarks. 'Take a seat. You can ask me anything you like.'

Sitting opposite him, I ask, 'What kind of work did you do for the Assembly?'

'Well.' Eustace pauses, scratching his head. 'I was an engineer.'

'Did you work on the tunnels in Folkshore?' I ask, holding my breath. 'Do any of the tunnels lead out of Folkshore?'

Eustace doesn't respond, but grabs his cane and hobbles to the corner of the room. *What's he doing?*

Reaching behind his wardrobe, Eustace removes a long, wide cardboard tube and wipes away the dust on it.

He beckons me over, then pulls out a rolled-up piece of

paper from the tube. With a steady hand, Eustace smooths the creases out of some blueprints. 'This is prime goods. These are the *original* blueprints of Folkshore, and they show every single tunnel in this place.' Eustace fishes his glasses from his trouser pocket and positions them on his face. 'You see this point here. If you go under the station, you come through a door and out onto one of the platforms.'

It's the entrance Prince used.

'And is there any other way out?' I ask.

'No, ma'am.' Eustace pounds his cane twice on the floor. 'I only know of one way in and one way out of Folkshore, but if you had *The Chronicles of Folkshore* scroll, it would set you on the right path.'

'Is it a scroll or a book?'

Eustace lowers his voice. 'It takes on many forms. When the first settlers came to Folkshore, one man kept the scroll by his lamp... the lamp began to quiver and shake and change shape.'

Is he going to tell me that the lamp gave him three wishes too?

Eustace's face goes blank and unresponsive. *Is he having an episode?*

'Eustace,' I call out. 'Eustace, are you okay?'

Grandma Pat stirs in the chair. 'What's wrong?'

The light comes back into Eustace's eyes and he says, 'I'm fine. Don't fuss over me. You can hold on to the blueprints for your project.' He taps his nose. 'Keep them safe and for your eyes only.'

Chapter 10

'Late night, sweetie?' Cindy asks as she stirs some blue food colouring into a mixing bowl. 'Looks like you're about to fall asleep on that cake.'

The sponge cake does look soft enough for me to use as a pillow.

'Yeah, I was up studying.'

I spent most of the night studying Eustace's blueprints. I know he said there wasn't any other way out of Folkshore, but I have to try something.

'Sorry, I didn't realise we'd be this busy today,' Cindy says. 'We've got some orders in, and then we have to start baking the treats for the Folkshore market tomorrow. You know how crazy it can get.' Before I can ask her any more, she has moved away. 'And the town hall meeting is in a few hours, so we need to be quick.'

'A town hall meeting?'

Cindy looks at me funny and replies, 'Yes. Where have you been? It's been the talk of Folkshore for weeks now. Everyone is going to be there.'

'Oh, yeah,' I say, clicking my fingers. '*That* meeting. I forgot.'

And the prize for the worst performance in history goes to Fola Oduwole.

Coming in from the back, Maya whips a card out of her pocket and slides it across the counter. Picking up the card, I turn it over and shake my head. This girl.

Cinderella Asamoah
More cake for you. More money for us.

'Did you make this?' I ask, already knowing the answer.

Maya flicks imaginary dirt off her shoulder. 'I sprinkled some Maya magic on Mum's laptop—and *boom*.' She creates an imaginary explosion with her hands. 'Tell all your friends. I'm in business.'

'Okay, Miss Money-Maker.' Cindy giggles. 'You and your sister can start decorating the cake for dessert tonight.'

Maya hops off the stool and pats her pocket, which is full of cards. 'I'll go and think of more ideas in the back with my assistant.'

For the next few hours, we bake and serve customers who come into the bakery. Cindy and I are a machine—with a few faults because I swear I almost *did* fall asleep on one of the cakes.

Cindy grabs a rag and wipes the surfaces. The door dings and Cindy stops cleaning. A black man in a navy suit, polished black shoes and a fresh trim with a greying patch, strides towards the counter like he owns the place. Why does he look so familiar?

Cindy bares her teeth and hisses, 'What are you doing here?'

Has someone possessed her body?

A few customers turn to stare at the man. He's older, but he has Cindy's nose and eyes. Is this her dad? One customer pulls out a phone to take a picture of him.

He scowls. 'Cinderella, give me a chance to speak for once.'

When Cindy completely ignores him, the man's nostrils flare and he taunts her. 'I didn't raise you to be a bitter woman. You should know better. I've been trying for months to speak to you and to see my granddaughters. Frankly, your behaviour towards me is *very* insulting. You're being a nuisance, just like your mother.'

Why is he talking to her like this? One thing my dad taught us is how important family is.

Cindy scrunches the rag tightly in her hand. Is she going to punch him? If I could fight, I would back her.

'I'm *nothing* like her, and you know it.' Cindy's voice is thick with emotion. 'I will come and speak to you when I'm ready. Please leave.'

The girls' laughter streams through the open door, and Cindy's dad's face relaxes. 'Is that the girls? Can't I just see them for a min—'

'No.' Cindy cuts him off. 'I'm sure the pictures Anastasia sends will last you for now.'

A look of surprise flashes over his face before his mask is back. 'You need to show me some respect,' he seethes. 'If that's how it's going to be, I won't bother.'

He turns and marches out.

Cindy serves a customer as if she and her dad weren't beefing a minute ago. She doesn't mention what happened, and I don't bring it up. They're like Bisi and Mum times 50.

I try to cheer Cindy up by showing her the photos I took today. There are a few close-ups of Cindy's hands piping swirls onto a carrot cake, and a mid-shot as she paints petals onto little icing flowers with a small brush.

'I'll upload them for you.'

'You're so good at that,' Cindy says. 'Is that what you want to do for a career?'

'Yeah. I mean, no.' I sigh. 'I want to, but I think I'm gonna be a doctor.'

Licking some icing off her finger, Cindy replies, 'I know how it is. I'm a baker and my dad is old-school. He'd been raised to aim for the best and he wanted the best for us, but you must follow your own path. Don't drown in other people's expectations of you.' She claps her hands and announces to the bakery, 'We're closing in five minutes!'

The powder-blue town hall building stands out, with its wide Grecian columns and classic arched windows. I'm mesmerised by the white marble floors inside and art painted on the high ceilings.

'This way, honey,' Cindy says, pointing to a set of double doors.

The massive auditorium is packed with Folkshorians. Red's head pops up in the middle and she signals to us.

Cindy beams. 'Oh lovely, Red has saved us some seats.'

When we reach her, Red hands me a Samsung. 'It's Gran's old phone. She said it's in case you want to talk to her about anything else.'

I flip the phone around in my hand. It's better than having no phone, but I still can't call home, only people in Folkshore.

'Tell your grandma I said thank you.'

'Why did you go and see Eustace?' Red asks, her nose wrinkling.

'I needed to find out more about Folkshore.' I look at Ty and lower my voice. 'Why didn't you tell him about me?'

'The less people who know, the better, and Ty has a big mouth.'

Ty, who was looking distracted before, says, 'What did you say?'

He touches her neck and Red screeches. 'Your hands are cold, man. Get off me!' She laughs.

Ty kisses Red. While they're distracted, I scan the hall. I spot Prince with some of the skaters from the Undercroft, and Rap, up at the front, gesturing wildly to Westley, who is sitting next to her, his usual patient expression on his face.

Red says slyly, 'Ty said he's been seeing you around with Prince.'

My face grows hot as Ty laughs at me. 'It's not like that.'

'I knew it! I was right. I *told* you she likes white boys.' Ty holds out his hand. 'Where's my money, Red?'

Did he actually bet that I liked Prince?

'He's just helping me!'

'See!' Red exclaims as she slaps Ty's hand away. 'I don't owe you jack! She's not going out with him.'

'Whatever, man,' he mopes. 'You still owe money. I don't care.'

The atmosphere shifts in the room as the red side door opens. Members of the Assembly make their way down the steps and take their seats in front of the mics. There's Tabitha Khan, a South Asian woman in a double-breasted suit and kitten heels. Edward Hamilton, an older white man in a black suit and straight blond hair, styled to the side. The last man is Cindy's dad. Roland Danquah.

Cindy's dad is in the Assembly.

'How does the Assembly work then?' I ask Red.

'There are three boroughs in Folkshore—Folkshore South, North and East. The people vote in three representatives. Roland is our representation for Folkshore South.'

Westley stands up at the front of the hall, addressing everyone. 'Hello and thanks for coming. My name is Westley and I'll be chairing today's meeting. We're mainly here to discuss and get an update on the Assembly's regeneration plans. We'll give them a chance to speak first before asking any questions.'

Edward speaks into his mic first. 'The regeneration plans are progressing well.'

'Well, mi backfoot,' Red mutters beside me. Another woman nods in agreement.

'New apartment buildings are being built for all Folkshorians who wish to invest in Folkshore's future, and businesses are being renovated as we speak,' he continues. 'Those who have decided to sell and move on were compensated well.'

It doesn't sound right.

'When I used to live in south London, the council came talking about some regeneration, but it was a lie,' I murmur to Red. 'We ended up moving out.'

For years they'd been talking about investing in the area with new buildings, but rent prices went up and things in our area started to change. They neglected the people who stayed, until they finally left, then the council tore down our block of flats and replaced it with penthouse apartments. None of it was for us. We wouldn't have been able to afford to live there.

'We know how important community is to Folkshore, and we don't want to take away from that,' Tabitha explains in a nasal voice. 'We only want Folkshore to reach its highest potential. With the restrictions in place and everything that transpired a year ago, we're invested in protecting and rebuilding Folkshore. We are here beside you.'

'Thank you, Edward and Tabitha,' Roland says. 'As my fellow Assembly members have already said, we're invested in bettering Folkshore, but we wouldn't be here without all of you voting us in. We're standing together as one Folkshorian family.'

'If we're a family, why isn't anything being done about the missing people?' someone asks.

Roland leans in closer to the mic and fixes his tie. 'We should dispel these rumours now. Some Folkshorians willingly chose to take the money offered to them and leave Folkshore. People are *not* going missing.'

Cindy huffs. 'He's lying. Some of the missing people would *never* just up and leave.'

'The Assembly want to be completely transparent with you about this whole process,' Roland continues, 'and that is why we will be holding an exhibition here at the town hall, which will include presentations, 3D models of the refurbishments being made in Folkshore, information on our investors, forums for local business owners, Q&A sessions, and much more.'

The Assembly fully sound like 419ers who offer you four nights in Paris, but instead you get one night under the bridge in Peckham. But I can see that a lot of people here are buying what the Assembly are saying.

Why do I care anyways? The only thing I need to be worried about is finding a way out of Folkshore. I can't get distracted—not again.

'The floor is now open for residents to speak,' Westley calls.

Anna gets in there first. 'Anna Tsang from the *Folkshore Gazette*. There have been rumours about these so-called "investors" of yours. I researched Hightower, and the last place they "invested" in led to many diverse communities being displaced and increased rent prices, which members of those communities could not afford. What do you have to say about this?'

'That is preposterous.' Edward puffs out his chest. 'You have it all wrong, Ms Tsang.' He pronounces her name like it's a swear word. 'Hightower is investing *in* Folkshore. We're making Folkshore better *for* you. New apartments, new shops and new opportunities.'

There are few claps and head nods at what Edward is saying. It sounds too good to be true—because it probably is.

Rapunzel springs up from her seat, looking like she's ready to drag everyone in here. 'You're chasing away the people who built this place and made it what it is!'

'And we've listened to you and taken on board all of your feedback.' Tabitha addresses Rapunzel. 'If you come along to the exhibition tomorrow, you'll be able to see what we're doing for yourself.'

The meeting goes on like this for a while, but one thing is for sure: the Assembly will talk their way out of anything.

You can ask them 'what is 4 + 4?' and they will answer 'a triangle'.

As we file out of the hall, the attendance sheet for the exhibition is filling up with the names of curious Folkshorians who want to hear more about the Assembly's scams—I mean, plans. Rumpelstiltskin Gold makes an appearance outside the hall, greeting people who want to talk to him.

'Rumpel's kinda fit for an old bloke, and he's rich too,' Bran says, appearing beside me. 'Did you know he used to live at Greenwood when he was younger?'

When did she get here?

'Yeah, I saw his picture on the wall.'

Noticing Bran eyeing at him, Rumpelstiltskin approaches us with a smile as polished as his shoes.

'Ah, two young constituents.' Rumpelstiltskin puts his hands together like he's praying. 'How are you, Bran? And, Leah, was it?'

Belle, the furniture shop owner, approaches us and says, 'I'm so sorry to bother you. Rumpelstiltskin, I've had a chance to think, and your terms seem fair. Would you be able to review my tenancy agreement now? I don't trust what the Assembly are doing.'

'Excuse me, ladies. If you ever have any questions or have a community need, my door is always open.' Rumpel moves away with Belle to discuss her tenancy agreement.

Red, Ty and Prince leave with Rapunzel and Westley. I bet they're going to Rap's secret meeting. I could go and warn them about what happened to my family. After I've done that, then I'll be back on getting home. It's just one meeting.

'Bran, do you know where Rapunzel's secret meeting is?' I ask.

'It's not really a secret meeting, Wottie,' she replies.

I shake my head. 'Wait, why am I Watson? Does that mean you're Sherlock?'

'Yeah, cos I'm clearly the brains here. The meeting is at Pascal's house. Why do you wanna know?'

Chapter 11

Pascal lives in a small, but picturesque, detached cottage close to the library, with stone-coloured brick and a midnight-black roof. We creep around the front garden because the grass looks *way* too neat and I don't want to ruin it. I've talked myself out of this several times since we got here.

'Bran, promise you won't do anything silly,' I say.

I haven't known Bran for long, but I can already tell that she is Priya on steroids.

Bran lifts her perfectly threaded eyebrows at me.

'I just want to go into the meeting, say what I have to say about what happened when me and my family were living in main London, and leave.'

Bran chews her gum aggressively. 'Alright, I got it. Take it easy.'

I follow Bran through the unlocked gate at the side of the house. She lifts up a green porcelain cat ornament and removes a black key from under it.

'They can't hide nothin' from me,' she brags, holding up the brass key between her freshly painted white nails.

I frown. 'But I swear Pascal told you where the key was, though?'

'Still, Wottie,' Bran replies in a patronising tone. 'It's my killa instinct.'

I ignore her like I do Bisi when she thinks everyone is her personal servant.

Bran eases the door open and knocks down an umbrella, sending it crashing to the floor.

'Crap!' Bran shout-whispers.

'Are you trying to get us caught?'

The house is dark. Bran's heeled boots click against the floor as we enter the spacious kitchen. The glow from the fridge illuminates Bran's face as she takes a carton of orange juice out of the fridge. She pours herself a glass and drinks it all in one go.

'Doing detective work makes you thirsty.'

'Have you finished?' I ask, crossing my arms.

'Alright, Wottie. Calm down. You're always so serious,' she says, putting the glass into the sink. 'It's this way.'

We creep down the staircase through the door in the kitchen. A horrible feeling cramps my chest, like something bad is about to happen.

'Bran. Where exactly is this meeting?'

'It's in the wine cellar, but don't worry about it, babes. We can just slip in the back.'

When my foot hits the bottom of the stairs, I stop and Bran slams into me.

'Why'd you stop?' she asks.

Everyone's eyes are on us. If looks could kill, Bran and I would be dead. Rap glares at us from the front. We have interrupted her.

Red and Ty are trying, and failing, to hold in their laughter. Prince shakes his head and mouths, 'Bobby.' Cindy is the only helpful one, as she scoots over to make space for us to sit down.

'As I was saying, we've been out on the streets for months now trying to get people to listen,' Rap continues. 'But the town hall meeting shows they're not going to do anything about what's happening.'

'They said my sister sold her house and left,' a woman responds. 'But I *know* she wouldn't do that without telling me first.'

'We have to face facts—things haven't been right for a long time.' Rapunzel punctuates each word. 'It's *clear* that the Assembly are lying to us. They say those apartments are for us and they're 'reinvesting' in the community, but they're just words.'

The room is buzzing with energy. It's like there's an invisible electric cable weaving itself around the people sitting here as Rapunzel speaks.

'But it seems as though the Assembly do care about Folkshore,' another voice cries out.

'We *all* care, and that's why we're here.' Rapunzel smacks the back of her hand into her palm. 'We need to make our voices heard. They said they're working to 'make Folkshore great again', to bring back opportunities and end the restrictions, but I don't see anything. Do you?'

There are more mumbles from the room.

'We are Folkshore. The business owners, the community, the people.'

I can imagine this scene in a film. The part where the leader hypes everyone up and they're like, 'Yeah, let's do it. Let's defeat the enemy.' If it was me filming, I would get a close-up of Rapunzel because this low lighting creates a gritty atmosphere and I know it'll captivate anyone watching. So many emotions pass over her face—anger, determination and sadness. I would try to capture that, and then a wider shot of the cellar to get the different reactions in the room.

While there are many people nodding, some people still look unsure about what's going on, but Rapunzel is right.

'She's right,' I say.

Everyone turns to face me at the back, and I almost turn back too.

'When I grew up in London... in *main* London,' I start, 'a similar thing happened with the council there. They promised all these things, but they didn't keep their promises. They knocked the block down and built these expensive apartments. Rap is right. You *have* to say something if you can.'

Rap gazes at me. I think I can see a shred of respect in her eyes, but it must be the lighting.

She nods. 'We should go down to the exhibition...'

Then the ceiling trembles, like there's a stampede above us. Pascal leaves his seat at the front. 'I'm sorry. Let me go and check what's going on up—'

The door slams against the wall at the top of the staircase, and four police pigs come trotting down the stairs.

'Police! You're all under arrest.'

They handcuff Rap. She struggles against the painful ties, almost taking one of the pigs' eyes out.

The police pig grunts and hisses in Rap's ear, 'Watch yourself, miss.'

The cold metal handcuffs are slapped on my wrists next, and my stomach lurches. As I'm pulled upstairs, I look at the once neat lawn, now massacred by multiple hoof marks.

'Please,' Pascal moans, gesturing to his lawn. 'Can you go *around*? You're ruining it.'

'Get off me!' Bran shouts, spitting in one of the officers' faces.

'In you get,' an older police pig says to me before pushing down my head for me to get inside the police van full of people.

Ty swears and kicks the metal inside of the van while Cindy tries to calm him down. Prince is shoved in beside me.

'What are they even arresting us for?' Red rages. 'They don't have any grounds. This is why I want to be a lawyer. The police in Folkshore think they can do anything.'

The steel door slams shut. Since the windows are tinted, I can't even see where we're going.

'Who's got the girls?' I ask Cindy.

'Huh,' she replies, shaking herself out of a daze. 'I'm sorry. This is just crazy. I can't believe they're arresting us. Anastasia has the girls. I thought this was going to be a normal meeting like the others. The police have *never* shown up before.'

I lean back against the metal side of the van, and I space out. What are we even getting arrested for?

We come to a screeching halt and the harsh air hits my face as the door is yanked open and we're dragged out like criminals. Shivering, we're taken into a sea-green building with vertically painted white lines. The main area has matching chairs with a reception desk in the centre of the room. An officer behind the desk is having a heated conversation with a man.

'Excuse me, sir. Can you please calm down?' the officer says.

'No!' the man shouts, breathing heavily. 'I won't calm down. I won't! I've been trying to explain to your colleague for an hour that some... *creature* has killed my friend.' The man stabs at the protective glass between them. 'It... it was dark... and shaped like a person, but it was, like, misty...'

'Misty?'

'Yes! Like it was made of smoke—but... I could see its heart.' He points at his own chest. 'A *dying* heart...'

'So, this misty creature has a *heart*?' the police pig asks sceptically. 'Are you describing a Shrieker, sir? Let's move into a conference hub, shall we? And you can tell me exactly how a mythical creature killed your friend.' The police pig turns to his colleague and signals that he thinks the man is crazy. 'Right this way, sir.'

Their voices fade out as they move down the corridor into one of the teardrop-shaped hubs.

'You can't just hold us here.' Rap mutters from her chair. 'What are we being arrested for? Having meetings isn't illegal!'

One of the police pigs with a chunk missing from his right ear crouches down, getting right in Rap's face. It's the officer who arrested her.

'I know your kind has been plotting,' he spits.

'What do you mean, my *kind*?' Rap seethes and struggles in her chair, fighting to free her hands from the cuffs.

The officer's partner, a pig with a short black moustache, drags him away from Rap.

'Officer Levi. What do you think you're playing at?' he whispers harshly. 'You need to focus. We're only looking for an illegal whose name begins with F and O. They're linked to this group somehow.'

I freeze in my seat. It can't be a coincidence—but how did they find me?

The automatic doors open and Mal storms in with the dirtiest look on her face. 'I want to speak with your sergeant, now!'

Officer Levi trots forward to where Mal is standing and jeers, 'She's busy.'

'Get her out here now!' Mal shouts. 'Or I'll have the news crew swarming this place. Police arresting underage teens and other innocents without stating just cause and *without* a warrant?'

'You tell them, Mal,' Red hollers from her seat.

A stout police pig trots out, her hair tied up under a blue police hat. 'What's going on in here?' she asks and stiffens after seeing Mal. 'Not you again.'

'Yes, it's *me* again,' Mal replies pointedly. 'And it'll always be me when the police continue to break the law. Your officers entered Pascal's property without a warrant and arrested everyone.'

'Is this true?' the sergeant asks. 'Did you enter the property without a warrant?'

Officer Levi grunts. 'We had a tip-off and reason to believe that they were harbouring someone without the proper permissions to be in Folkshore.'

The sergeant advances slowly towards the police pig with the moustache. 'You're not answering my question, Officer Kelly. Did you have a warrant?'

'No, ma'am.' Officer Kelly bows his head. 'We didn't have one.'

The sergeant swears under her breath. 'You're all free to go. Release them.'

Officer Levi grunts.

'Now, please!' the sergeant booms.

The handcuffs are removed, release forms are signed, and we're all escorted out of the police station.

Officer Levi glowers at us from the automatic doors. 'We'll be watching you.'

I hear stomping behind me and Red's voice.

'Rap, calm down.'

Someone tugs at my arm, and spins me around.

Rap looks vexed. 'This is all *your* fault,' Rap barks. 'They were looking for *you*. How did they even know where we were?'

A few of the people from our group turn to see what's going on. I don't need more attention on me.

'I have no idea, but trust me, I swear I didn't say anything.'

'Trust you?' Rap mocks. 'I don't even know you. Stay away from us, snitch.'

Chapter 12

'You saw the way Mal just came in and told those pigs to do one.' Bran cackles as we leave Greenwood the next morning. 'And don't worry about Rap, she has a stick shoved right up her ass.'

I couldn't sleep all night because I was worried that either the police or Rap would get me. If I don't figure a way out quickly, they might catch me, and then what will happen?

'We shouldn't have gone to that meeting,' I reply.

I shouldn't have gotten on the train to Folkshore, and I can't even tell Bran the whole truth because she doesn't know who I really am.

'Who are you then?' she asks. 'Are you a spy?'

'What?' I ask, confused.

'Prince was right,' she replies, popping her gum. 'You do need to work on that talking out loud thing. Are you two going out?'

'We're not.' I choke. 'It's not like that.'

Bran prods me in the arm, like I'm a science experiment gone wrong. 'Are you like one of those nuns who keep it chained up until marriage?' she asks. 'There's nothing wrong with it, babes.'

'I'm not a nun, but I only want to be with someone like *that* when I'm married.' I shrug. 'And I have something to tell you, Bran. Rap is annoyed at me because I'm the reason everyone got arrested yesterday.'

'What are you on about, Wottie?'

Looking Bran dead in the eyes, I repeat what I said. 'I'm the reason all of you got arrested. The police were looking for me because I'm not from Folkshore and my name's not Leah. It's Fola.'

Bran throws her head back and laughs as her hair whips crazily in the breeze, creating a dark scarf around her neck. 'I know who you are, Wottie. You're a bad liar and your boyfriend, Prince, told me. You know he can't keep anything from me.'

'I'm not a bad liar.' I huff, but we both know the truth.

The high street is packed to the brim with market stalls.

'Later, Fols.' Branna struts down the street, hollering at people as she goes.

'Thank God you're here!' Cindy squeaks and throws an apron at me as I push open the door of the bakery.

Cindy looks stressed. Her hair is caked in flour and she's attacking the batter with a wooden spoon. 'There's so much to do!' she shouts and discards the wooden spoon, causing batter to splash onto the counter. 'Yesterday was ridiculous. I mean, who do those police officers think they are? Do you know that Anastasia almost called my father? Imagine his smug face when he hears about what happened to us! And now we're behind for the market.'

'We can do this.' Tightening the apron strings around my waist, I focus all my attention on helping Cindy. 'I'll make the brownies.'

Yesterday was my fault; I won't ruin the market too. After what feels like hours, we finish everything on Cindy's list. It's like she's feeding the 5,000.

We plate all the sweet treats onto fancy three-tier cake stands. Cindy places a spare tray in between us with all the leftovers that didn't quite make it. I ignore the chocolate fudge brownies, the white chocolate blondies and the lemon drizzle slices, and go straight for the red velvet cake. The cake crumbles on my tongue and does a little dance.

I don't realise Cindy is watching me until I hear a snicker.

'At least I know what's your favourite now, so I can make extras,' she says. 'Do you not like the others?'

I point to the brownie, the blondie and the lemon drizzle. 'That's Bisi's favourite, Roti's and the lemon drizzle is Deji's.'

Cindy sips her tea. 'Are they your siblings?' she asks.

'Yeah.'

Even though I don't think our house is big enough for all of us, I still miss them—even my mum, with all her drama.

'If you miss your family, why don't you give them a call?' Cindy asks, as if it's the easiest thing to do. 'Don't be like me and leave things to fester.'

'I want to,' I reply. 'Especially my brother, Deji.'

For months I've been trying to ignore the fact that he's

having the surgery because I'd googled the risks then wished I hadn't.

'Are you okay, honey?' Cindy asks.

'No, I'm not.' I hesitate. 'My brother is having surgery to remove a tumour. He has cancer.'

She touches my shoulder. 'I'm so sorry, bug. I hope the surgery goes well.'

'I hope so too.'

Cindy slides me a white envelope over the counter. 'Here, this is for you.'

Picking up the sealed envelope, I use my index finger to tear it open. A small, folded note rests on a few bank notes.

Dear Leah,

Here's your pay for all your hard work. Thanks so much for the help, sweets. You're a lifesaver.

Cindy x

They are Folkshorian notes. Instead of the Queen, there's an image of the Hometree on their money.

'Thanks, Cindy.'

'My pleasure. Time to get out there.' Cindy picks up two of the cake stands. 'Can you carry that one out? My little shopkeeper and my big scammer are waiting for us.'

The street is teeming with spices and colour. The first stall has an array of foods that I can recognise with my eyes closed. Okra is stacked in a little basket beside a tower of ripe yellow plantains, yams, bunches of spinach, sweet peppers and Scotch bonnets.

'Hello, darling.' A short black woman with deep cuts on her cheeks appears from nowhere. Her lips shimmer with silver lipstick. 'You want to buy anything?'

'No, Auntie,' I reply. 'I'm just looking.'

She grins wider. 'Where are you from? Ṣé o gbọ́ Yorùbá?'

'Yes, I do understand Yoruba.' I smile back.

She nods. 'Kí ni ò ń ṣe níbí? You helping your friend?' She looks at Cindy, who is hovering behind me.

'Yes, Auntie. Her stall's further down.'

'Okay, darling,' Auntie replies. 'I'm Winnie. Come back and see me if you want something.' She flashes me a smile and disappears.

'It's great that you can speak Yoruba,' Cindy says. 'I can't speak a bit of Twi.'

Cindy's stall has floral bunting hanging off the edge of the table, a pink patterned tablecloth, and rotating cake stands.

'Mum!' Dani calls, running over to hug her mum's legs.

A few customers wander over, the smell of Cindy's cakes drawing them in. The phone Grandma Pat gave me buzzes in my pocket.

Red

> Are you going to the exhibition?

I pocket my phone and serve the customers. My hands get sore from the number of cakes and treats I pack.

'Why don't you take a quick break?' Cindy asks, watching me. 'We've got it from here.'

I look at the message from Red again and respond to Cindy, 'I'll be back in 15 minutes.'

If I go to the exhibition, I can see once and for all if the Assembly are telling the truth or scamming everyone.

The main foyer of the town hall has a large buffet table stretching from one end to the other. They even have 3D rendering of what Folkshore's high street could look like with refurbishments and upgrades to all the shops.

Anna Tsang sulks beside me, holding a champagne flute. 'This is absolutely ridiculous.'

'What is?' I ask.

'All of this.' She gestures to the room. 'They're obviously trying to dazzle the residents to hide the truth. If people *knew* who those investors really were, they would be running away from here.'

'I agree with you,' I reply. 'I think the Assembly are definitely hiding something. There's a story here.'

Anna pivots so she's facing me. 'You know, you remind me of myself. A young, hungry journalist. Here.' She hands me her business card. 'If you ever need access to the *Folkshore Gazette*'s archives to do some digging, stop by and I can get you intern access.'

'Thank you.'

'Is that Hansel over there?' Anna is talking to herself now. 'I can get a quote from him.'

I tuck the card into my pocket and watch Anna whizz across the room to corner Hansel.

The exhibition stretches down the powder-blue halls. Folkshore does have some beautiful buildings. I climb up winding marble steps to even more rooms showcasing Folkshore's history. The photographs go as far back as the 1800s and the first settlers in Folkshore.

I pause at one photograph in particular because there is something off about it. It is a picture of the current Assembly members standing in front of the town hall but, when I look closely, I notice that the lighting is off and the number of shadows don't match.

My fingers touch the photo, and there's a clicking noise. The wall behind the photograph moves to reveal stairs.

I step away, but the sound of a familiar voice has me moving back towards the stairs. Roland. What is he doing up there?

I creep up the stairs and pause once I reach the top. The room is open plan with an office in the centre. The door is slightly ajar.

All the Assembly members and Rumpel sit around a glass table. When all their heads turn towards me, I dive behind a desk to hide, and bump my knee against its hard corner. I almost cry out at the sharp pain coursing through my knee.

'Everything seems to be going to plan with this whole regeneration scheme,' Edward says.

I reach up and set my camera at the corner of the table to record what they're saying.

'I heard some chatter about a possible mole coming into Folkshore. We don't need another Jack issue.'

Do they think I'm a mole?

Wasn't Jack charged for killing an Assembly member and selling Folkshore's secrets? They probably think I'm going to expose Folkshore.

'We need to deal with that as soon as possible,' Rumpel snaps. 'I can't have any bad business attached to my name again. I've barely recovered from the Reckoning debacle.'

'Well, it's funny, isn't it, Rumpel?' Edward asks in a snide tone. 'Usually you're on top and you know everything.'

'It's peculiar how the muzzled pup thinks he can bite,' Rumpel mutters back, shutting Edward up.

'Let's just stick to the plan,' Roland says. 'Do we need to worry about Folkshore's climate? It's getting worse every day.'

'I'm sure it'll settle soon,' Tabitha reassures him. 'Don't buy into that outdated, misinformed report about the spectral phenomena of Folkshore. The report is wrong. Folkshorians don't control Folkshore—*we* do, and there's no evidence of this so-called 'white light' or 'Lx20' in Folkshorians. We bleed red like everyone else. We are *not* being exposed to 'toxins'. Listen to me. Our regeneration scheme will work. *We* control Folkshore; not the people, nature or its creatures.'

Slapping the table, Edward adds, 'Good because we cannot risk upsetting the investors again. Do you know how many people have already secured their place here? Folkshore will be Silverkeep 2.0. Just look how well the regeneration scheme worked in Whitemount—and it doesn't have *half* of the potential Folkshore has.'

'And what about all the missing people?' Roland asks.

Edward snorts. 'We have more pressing issues. If it becomes a real problem, then we can look into it.'

'Let's wrap up this meeting,' Rumpel says. 'I have another appointment soon.'

Using that as my cue, I switch off my camera and slip out of the room. I creep back down the stairs and into the main exhibition, then sneak out the entrance as if I was never there. I knew there was something off about that regeneration scheme.

I'm almost back at the market when the ground starts to shake violently. The cement cracks down the middle of the street like an egg.

Chapter 13

The furniture store owner, Belle, pulls me inside her shop and I dive under the nearest table. I'm not the only one here. My fingernails dig into the table leg. I squeeze my eyes shut, bow my head, and pray everyone survives as the thunderous noise shakes the foundations of the shop and items crash to the floor.

After some time, the trembling stops.

'Everyone okay?' Belle yells.

The furniture shop is destroyed. Stepping through the broken furniture on shaky legs, I come out onto the high street, speechless when I see the amount of damage the earthquake has caused.

Do we need to worry about Folkshore's climate? It's getting worse every day.

Tabitha said it would settle down soon, but look at Folkshore. The tree bark is all cracked and the trees are leaking a luminous liquid.

My Converses squash through plantain from Auntie Winnie's stall. There's movement under a collapsed market stall, and I recognise Auntie Winnie's red Adidas trainers. As she groans and struggles to get up, I see that a piece of wood has punctured her leg. Blood is seeping out. I use my coat to apply pressure to the wound, and Auntie cries out in pain.

'Help!' I shout.

Cindy scrambles through the debris towards us with Maya, Dani and Anastasia following. Cindy's and Anastasia's faces are covered in scratches, but the girls are unharmed.

'Are you hurt?' Cindy asks, searching for where the blood is coming from. 'Where is my phone? I need to call the ambulance.'

'Mum.' Maya points to the phone in Cindy's hands.

'Thanks, sweetie.' Cindy dials the number for the ambulance. 'Leah, can you go and get the first-aid kit from the bakery? If it's still in one piece. It's in the corner by—'

'By the clean cloths,' I finish.

Cindy's hands overlap mine as she applies pressure to Auntie Winnie's leg. A tickle works its way up my throat, and I sneeze a few times as I stumble through the debris, passing dazed Folkshorians. The front windows of the bakery are shattered, but the rest of the bakery has survived. My shoes crunch on broken glass as I enter. I spot the orange pack lodged under the counter.

With the first-aid kit tucked in my hand, I run back towards the group, but a shriek from Once Upon a Time Street makes me pause. I've heard that sound before.

I sneak into the side street—then I have another vision. It's different from the last. It's not blurry. Streams of blue lightning from the Hometree connect with the sky, widening a black hole which begins swallowing up everything and everyone. Fear flavours the air as a group of Shriekers claw their way out of Folkshore's tunnels, gliding over dead Folkshorians. Rap, Red, Prince, Cindy and Bran lie motionless on the street.

In an instant, the vision is gone and I'm standing here, shivering at what I saw in my head. They were all dead.

In the middle of Once Upon a Time Street, a man with a metal device stuck in his chest is struggling; his legs kick restlessly like a baby. Stooping over him is a misty black shadow shaped like a human. A Shrieker. I thought they weren't real. I cup my mouth to muffle my scream.

The Shrieker's shadowy hands are fastened on the metal device, which is collecting white light from the man's chest. The light flows into a large vial attached to the end of the device. The Shrieker licks some of the white liquid that drips on the ground.

As I step back, the Shrieker's head snaps round to look at me. My gaze locks on to its white, misty eye sockets. It stands up, ripping the metal device out of the man's chest. Droplets of blood splatter on his clothes.

Fragments of the Shrieker's misty body evaporate as it glides towards me. Through its murky body, a black, decaying heart beats irregularly, shuddering.

If Mum was here, she would've been praying and throwing anointing oil at the Shrieker.

My phone rings.

The Shrieker's hands cup its ears to block the noise out. It flares its misty lips, and spirals of black smoke crawl out of the Shrieker's mouth, winding together in the air as it shrieks again.

The ambulance's siren makes the Shrieker scamper off. Deliriously, I stumble back towards the main road to find a paramedic.

'Help!' I cry out.

'Miss, are you hurt?' one of the paramedics asks.

'No, I'm fine.' I gulp, pointing to Once Upon a Time Street. 'But there's a man there...'

'Leave it with me,' she replies, moving in that direction.

I pray he isn't dead.

The first-aid kit is still tucked under my armpit when I reach Cindy and the others.

'Are you okay?' Cindy asks. Her voice barely rises above the ringing in my ears. 'The ambulance is here.'

The paramedic lifts Auntie Winnie into the ambulance on a stretcher.

Cindy's smooth hand grabs mine, but I can barely feel it.

'Sweetie, can you hear me?'

Chapter 14

Lying on my back, I stare up at the white ceiling in my room. I can't close my eyes. Every time I do, I either see the vision or the Shrieker attacking that man. It's his screams and those haunting white eye sockets.

Red slurps on the chicken soup Grandma Pat made me because she heard I was sick after the earthquake. 'Fola, you should eat some of this.'

'Leave her alone, Red Riding Hood,' Bran says.

'My name is Red,' she snaps.

I roll over in my bed to face them. 'Remember you told me before about those Shriekers? Do you think they could be real?'

Everything that *should* be impossible in Folkshore seems to be possible, so why not this too?

Red laughs into the soup, but her laughter dies away when she sees my face. 'No, they're not real. My grandma told me about them to scare me, that's all.'

Prince's black Vans appear by my open door. 'How ya feelin', Fola?'

Bran winks. 'You here to make her feel better, Charming?'

'I want to go home.' I sulk.

When I don't offer anything else, Prince slides down the wall onto the carpet with a sketchpad in his hands.

I drift off and wake up to a stiff right arm and an empty room. I need to go home. I don't care how, but I can't stay here. If the police aren't after me, then I'm seeing those demonic creatures. I need to get away.

Something thumps against my door. My heart leaps.

'Who's there?' I ask, clutching my Converse as a weapon.

Prince swears.

I poke my head out the door. Prince is chasing a runaway spray can down the hall and his black jeans have ridden up to reveal his giraffe boxers.

'I didn't know you liked giraffes like that,' I tease.

'Clown.' Prince immediately tugs down his hoodie and turns around with the can in his hand. 'You seem better. I want to show you something.'

'Show me what?'

I hope Prince isn't one of those serial killers I keep telling Pree about because he's not luring me nowhere.

Prince howls with laughter before remembering that it's almost midnight and everyone is asleep.

'I cross my heart,' he says, fingers marking his chest. 'I'm not going to kill ya. Bring your baby along witcha.'

I have been stuck in this room for ages—it would be good to go out. Kicking off the fluffy white slippers Bran bought for me, I put on my trainers and snatch my bag from the chair.

The streets of Folkshore are quiet and the trees are

healing themselves right in front of my eyes, as if an invisible doctor is stitching up the cracks in their bark.

Rubble is piled at the side of the high street. Folkshore's construction workers have started to clear the streets.

'Prince, what do you know about the Shriekers?'

'Are they comin' to getcha?' Prince asks, humour swimming in his icy eyes. 'Shriekers are *supposedly* trapped in the tunnels under Folkshore. They can't escape.'

That can't be right.

'Why'd you ask?'

Itching the back of my neck, I try to come up with an answer. 'I just wondered.'

'Mmhmm,' Prince replies as he wiggles his fingers near me. 'Beware of the Shriekers.'

I kiss my teeth and push him away. 'Whatever.'

He chuckles. 'This way.'

We turn off on Godmother Street and go around the back of an orange-rusted building.

'Promise I'm still not trying to kill you or nothin'.'

'Alright, but you're going in first,' I reply, raising my chin.

Prince heaves the steel door open before stepping inside. I pull the heavy door closed behind me. The sound ricochets through the empty warehouse.

'What is this place?' I ask.

At first, it just appears to be a large, wide open space, but as I step further in, small beams of light dart in through the holes in the corroded skyline. The walls are covered in the same moving graffiti, which tells a thousand stories.

'Prince, what is this place?' I repeat, turning back to him.

I pause in front of one piece, as it seems more personal than the others. I watch an expressionless man stumbling along, a parasite growing in his stomach. By the end of the way, the parasite has completely consumed the man and he's unrecognisable.

'I found this place a few years ago after we came back to Folkshore from Ireland.'

'So, you haven't always lived in Folkshore?'

'Naw—I was born here, we went back to Ireland to live with family for a bit, and then we came back here cos my ma wanted us to be settled in one place.'

I can't believe that I didn't connect the dots before. 'It's you, isn't it? It's your graffiti that's all over Folkshore.'

He nods.

'You're *very* talented.'

'Cheers.'

Prince drops his bag to the floor with a clank, while I stare at the moving art some more.

'How does it move like that?'

'Findin' Folkshore is how. When I was younger, my ma was always sayin' *you'll find whatever drives your soul.* He laughs humourlessly. 'I mean, in between helping my da, I'd sketch, but nothin' like this. This...' He points to the art. 'This happened after most of my family were killed in that car accident.'

Most of his family died. What am I supposed to say to that?

'I'm *so* sorry.'

'Thanks.' Prince kneels down, unzips his mysterious bag, and pulls out a few spray cans. I guess he's done talking.

He shakes a can and starts working on a new piece. I do the thing that seems most natural to me. Lifting the camera to my eye, I do what I'm great at.

Imagine if I could do this properly and not think about my parents. Being behind the camera is the only time I feel like me.

I don't know how long we stay like this, but the sound of Prince's empty cans hitting the cold warehouse floor brings me back to the present. His new piece is not finished yet, but it's a moving mural of his family.

Before shrugging on his hoodie, Prince fixes the peeling cling film covering a tattoo on his arm.

Pointing at it, I ask, 'What tattoo did you get?'

Removing the cling film, he twists around to show me. 'It's an old one, but I added to it.'

The tattoo is a tally with 12 marks.

'What are the marks for?'

'How many months it's been since I've seen my brother, Noah.'

'Is that who you were trying to see in London?'

Prince hesitates for a second. 'Yup. When the accident happened, up in main London, they took Noah away to foster care. I'd come home to sort things out before going back to join him, but the Reckoning happened, and then life happened. At least they treat him good up there. Let's get back before Mal catches on.'

Instead of going back the way we came, we end up passing an old church. Nature has engulfed the outside, so it's more leaves than building. When I found out that Deji was sick, I struggled with my faith because how could someone like Deji get sick? It's not right.

I'm drawn to the church. 'I'll be two minutes.'

I push open the chipped door, leaving Prince outside rolling a cigarette. The church is deserted, as I thought it would be. I wait to feel connected to God again, but all I can hear is Deji telling me to stop sulking and to fight the Shriekers.

There's a woman sitting further down the bench. She nuzzles deeper into her thick blue shawl. The silence doesn't last long; Rap stomps in with her smaller shadow, who *has* to be her sister, following her.

I duck down so she doesn't see me.

'Mum. Where'd you go?' Rap scolds the woman. 'I've been looking for you everywhere, and Cassandra was scared. You know that people have been going missing.'

Rap's mum laughs softly, and the vein on Rap's head looks ready to burst.

'I was only gone for an hour, Rapunzel,' she replies. 'I wasn't leaving you.'

Rap's voice echoes across the church. 'I always have to do everything!'

'And who told you to do everything, mmm?'

'Who else is going to do it then?' Rap asks.

'If you take a pause and breathe, the world won't suddenly

collapse because you're not out to save it.' Her mum shifts in her seat. 'You know that on the day you were born, they gave you to me—'

'And I was the most beautiful baby ever,' Rap interrupts. 'My hair was so soft and curly and long like Rapunzel's. Yeah, I know.'

Rap's mum continues as if she hadn't spoken. 'And from that day I knew I'd do anything for you. Sit down.'

Reluctantly, Rap sits down beside her mum and waits for her to speak.

'Yes, there were times in the past when I wasn't at my best, but that was many years ago, Rapunzel. You can trust now that I won't let you or Cassandra down.' Rap's mum gets up from the bench, taking Cassandra's hand, and leaves the church. I assume they've gone, so I raise my head, but I was wrong.

Rap stands there, holding her mum's shawl. Can she see me?

Rap cocks her head to the side. 'Of course I can see you.'

'I didn't snitch,' I reply. 'I swear I don't know how the police knew where we were, but there *is* something going on with the Assembly—and I have proof.'

Chapter 15

'What is she doing in my house?' Red asks, pointing at Bran, who's strutting through Red's living room like she owns the place.

'*She* has a name, Red Riding Hood,' Bran shoots back.

Bran plants herself on Grandma Pat's plastic-covered sofa, while Rap holds Red back from fighting Bran.

Ty comes back into the room, confused. 'What happened? I was only gone for, like, ten seconds.'

In the corner of the room, Prince chuckles into his sketchpad.

'Why did you bring us here?' Rap asks me impatiently. 'Where's your proof about the Assembly?'

I hold out the camera for Rap to take, and she plays the video for everyone to hear.

'*Everything seems to be going to plan with this whole regeneration scheme.*'

Bran pops her cherry-flavoured gum. 'Isn't that Edward?'

'*I heard some chatter about a mole coming into Folkshore. We don't need another Jack issue.*'

At hearing the word 'mole', Rap throws me a harsh look, like I knew she would.

'Just keep listening,' I respond.

'Let's just stick to the plan. Do we need to worry about Folkshore's climate? It's getting worse every day.'

'I'm sure it'll settle soon,' Tabitha reassures him. *'Don't buy into that outdated, misinformed report about the spectral phenomena of Folkshore. The report is wrong. Folkshorians don't control Folkshore— we do, and there's no evidence of this so-called 'white light' or 'Lx20' in Folkshorians' blood. We bleed red like everyone else. We are not being exposed to 'toxins'. Listen to me. Our regeneration scheme will work. We control Folkshore; not the people, nature, or its creatures.'*

'Good, because we cannot risk upsetting the investors again. Do you know how many people have already secured their place here? Folkshore will be Silverkeep 2.0. Just look how well the regeneration scheme worked in Whitemount—and it doesn't have half of the potential Folkshore has.'

'Folkshore looks *nothing* like Silverkeep,' Red comments.

'Where is Silverkeep?' I ask.

'It's another hidden place in Switzerland.' Red types on her phone and shows me an image of Silverkeep—a modern version of Folkshore with the exact same apartments.

'I knew it!' Ty exclaims. 'My friend was saying that those apartments are connected to the missing people. Shamia went missing after she went to see one.'

Red looks pointedly at him. 'Ty, I saw Shamia yesterday and she was fine. I don't think this audio is enough proof.'

'What more do you need?' Bran asks. 'The Assembly are

making Folkie into bloody Silverkeep. Silverkeep! That place with even posher twats.'

'And what about all the missing people?'

Rap clenches her jaw at all the interruptions. 'Can everyone be quiet so I can hear?'

'We have more pressing issues. If it becomes a real problem, then we can look into it.'

'What does he mean, a 'real problem'?' Rap fumes. 'It's *already* a real problem!' She tosses my camera towards me. I catch it because I can't afford a new camera.

Rap paces in her Doc Martens. 'I can't *believe* this.'

'You're mashing up my grandma's carpet,' Red says. 'As I said before, we need more evidence.'

Prince cracks his knuckles, discarding his sketchbook. 'How do we get it?'

The investigative documentaries I love come to mind because they expose information concealed by people in power. People like the Assembly.

'We can try to get more evidence against the Assembly,' I propose. 'And then we can share it in, like, a short documentary to expose what's happening and to inform all the Folkshorians.'

'It could work,' Rap muses, 'But we need a plan.'

'What about if we check one of the shops? If they're making Folkshore into Silverkeep 2.0, then maybe they've already started changing the shops. Cindy mentioned Leonard. His antique shop is covered in plastic sheets and scaffolding.'

'Yes,' Red agrees. 'That's smart.'

'Oh, and I almost forgot about this.' I dig out Anna's card from my pocket and explain what happened. 'We can try and find something in their records.'

We spend the next hour planning. When I say 'planning', I mean that Ty shouted about beating up the Assembly members and Bran wanted to join him. Then Rap complained about how stupid their idea was and Red explained how many years they'd get in prison for that crime. Oh, and Prince attempted to note our 'plans' down in his sketchpad.

'We all know what we need to do, right?' Rap says. 'Don't do anything dumb.' She glares at Ty, who has spent most of the time figuring out how to get the Assembly back.

Ty's casual grin slips off his face as his eyebrows furrow. 'I'll do what I want. Look what they're tryna do.'

'I hate what they're doing too,' Rap spits, 'but we have a plan now. So, just stick to it, alright?'

About 20 minutes later, we're hiding in a corner near the high street. The police pigs are trotting all over the place.

'How long are we gonna hide here?' Bran whines. 'I'm going.'

'Bran, wait,' I say, but she's already dashing across the street, narrowly missing the police.

'Look at her struttin' over there like a fecking peacock,' Prince whispers.

Ty shakes his head. 'And you thought *I* would be the problem, yeah.'

Rap mumbles something about 'crazy white girl' as we creep through the streets to Leonard's shop.

'It's locked,' Bran states, tugging at the door.

'You got a comb in that bag of yours, Fola?' Prince asks.

Reluctantly, I hand over my fine-toothed comb and watch in horror as Prince jams the pointed edge into the lock. 'Don't break it!'

He twists the comb back and forth for a few seconds. 'Gotcha,' he exclaims and pushes the door open.

'This is illegal,' Red warns us. 'Do you know this is trespassing? We could be sued.'

'You said we needed evidence, Red,' Rap replies. 'The door is already open. It'll be a waste.'

Red relents, sighing. 'Only for a minute and then we have to leave.'

It is not an antique shop any more. Taking my camera out, I film the light blue pond on either side of the walkway. Pink petals and lotus candles float in it. Wooden slats cover the walls, and the ceiling has spotlights. I zoom in to read the glass sign—*Evergreen Rejuvenation Spa*—and pull Bran back at the last minute from dipping her foot in the pond.

'You what?' Bran exclaims. 'They're charging £72 to put shit on your face.'

The treatments here are strange, and the prices are even worse.

Devil's Kiss

———✺———

Open flames procedure to rejuvenate cells in skin.

The Sting of Life

———✺———

Bees trapped in a cocoon to sting face, which stimulates elasticity.

Faecal Fantasies

———✺———

A rare mixture of canary droppings, grain and water lathered on to the face for exfoliation.

Van Helsing

———✺———

Blood is extracted from your leg and reinjected into your face to boost collagen production.

Ty comes back into the room licking a strawberry Cornetto that he didn't come in with. 'They have a freezer back there.'

We all stop dead as a torch beam shines in through the gaps in the wooden slats.

'Are you sure you heard something?' a police pig asks her colleague. 'Do you want me to go in and check it out?'

Chapter 16

'It's good... we split up... they would've caught us,' I gasp, holding on to a wall near the *Folkshore Gazette* building, which has a giant, pink satellite dish.

We've previously established that my body is allergic to any form of physical activity.

'You won't catch me doing anything like that ever again,' Red moans, clutching her side. 'I've got a stitch.'

'Why are you both breathing like that?' Rap stares at us in disgust as she stands there with not a single drop of sweat on her head. 'We only ran for a minute.'

'Do you remember what happened the last time we were here, Rap?' Red asks.

Rap nods. 'Our first protest.'

After seeing my confused face, Red explains, 'Our teacher, Mr Phillips, was discriminating against us, which is unlawful cos of the Equality Act. Anyways, the school wasn't listening so me and Rap got some other students. We refused to go back to lessons until they took us seriously. Lizzie from the *Folkshore Gazette* invited us down here to talk about what happened.'

Rachel Faturoti

The inscriptions on the side of the building make sense now. *News for the people. Truth for the people.*

'What happened afterwards?' I ask.

'Mr. Phillips changed schools,' Rap replies.

It's as if she's talking about going to the shop and buying bread, not doing something and *actually* making a difference. The most I've done is get straight As.

The inside of the *Folkshore Gazette* matches the outside, except there's a preppy blonde woman behind a turquoise desk, using a headset.

'Hi, I'm here to see Anna Tsang.'

The lady tilts her head at me like she's draining water out of her right ear and offers us a rigid smile. 'Unfortunately, Ms Tsang is not in the building.'

Fishing Anna's business card from my pocket, I flip it around and spot a mobile phone number on it.

Red takes the card from me. 'Lemme try to call her.'

The receptionist types on her keyboard. 'Is there anyone else I can call from the *Folkshore Gazette*?'

'Lizzie Mensah,' Rap responds impatiently.

'Here I am. Long time no see, ladies.' A short black woman strides towards us in a red peplum pencil dress and honey-coloured micro braids. She hugs Rap and Red. 'How can I help you ladies?'

'We're here to see Anna,' I reply. 'She was going to give me intern access to look through the *Folkshore Gazette* archives for a project I'm doing.'

Lizzie's smile drops and she lowers her voice so only we

can hear her. 'Anna didn't show up for work this morning. People are saying that she may have gotten caught in the earthquake, but Anna's part of town wasn't hit badly. I've known her for five years and she's *never* missed a day of work, which is probably unhealthy, but still. I'm hoping it's just a bad day and she's okay.'

Lizzie's phone beeps in her hands and she looks at it nervously. 'I'm going to take all of you down to the archive room, but you can't be there too long because I have another meeting, and we're not supposed to leave people down there unsupervised.' Her phone beeps again and she sighs. 'Sorry about that—it's my boss updating us on the investigations. The newspaper has been getting these threatening messages for weeks, and we don't know where Anna is. Everyone's on edge.'

Demonic creatures, unstable weather, missing people, a lying council, and someone sending threats. What *doesn't* this place have?

We pile into the wide lift, which descends into an underground storeroom where Lizzie scans her badge by a set of reinforced double doors.

There are three computers at the front of the room.

'Here's the login for the computerised records so you can find the articles organised by year.' Lizzie's phone beeps again. 'I've got to take this, but I'll be back.'

Shaking the mouse to wake it, I search 'the Assembly'. Hundreds of articles come up. I send them to the printer.

'Wait, Ty. I'm going to put you on loudspeaker.' Red clicks

her fingers to get my attention. She's sitting at a computer at the far end of the room. 'Say what you said again, Ty.'

'I heard that the pigs are offering 2k for any information on that mole they're looking for,' he says.

'Alright, I'll speak to you later,' Red replies, ending the call. 'You need to stay away from the police, Fola.'

My skin begins to itch. They're offering £2,000 just for information about me. 'Trust me, I don't want to go anywhere near them.'

Bran

> Asked Mal for her mate's
> number from Whitemount

> I tried it but it's unavailable

Me

> Thanks x

Another dead end.

I enter other keywords into the database: 'the Assembly + the Reckoning'.

A video file appears at the bottom of the screen, titled 'Jack Crombie's interrogation'. I click on it. Jack sits in front of two police officers in an interrogation room.

'I swear to you, I've told you everything! I didn't try to expose Folkshore's secrets, and I definitely didn't kill Duke. He... he was my friend.' Jack weeps.

'We have evidence and witnesses who say otherwise, sir.'

'*The Assembly are liars! They're all liars.*' I actually believe what Jack is saying.

Their archives seem to have information on everything. My fingers immediately type '*The Chronicles of Folkshore*'.

An article from over a year ago comes up. I scan the Arts and Entertainment section describing an auction for the tablet. *It really does take many forms.*

Rumpelstiltskin Gold bids £10,000 for the Chronicles of Folkshore *tablet...*

£10,000! Why would someone bid that much for a tablet?

'I actually found it!' Red calls out and we rush to crouch by her.

Sighing, Rap straightens and flicks Red's screen. 'We're supposed to be looking for evidence. What is this?'

Red glares at Rap. 'Look. I think I found the report Tabitha was talking about in Fola's recording. I used the keywords search. It's called 'An investigation into the spectral phenomena of Folkshore'. It's the same report. I know it.' Long black boxes block out most of the sentences. 'They've redacted the report to stop us from reading their secrets.'

'Print it,' Rap commands.

Red grumbles, clicking fiercely on the printer icon. 'I was going to anyway.'

Lizzie steps out of the lift and calls out, 'Girls! I'm sorry, but it's time to go. The police are here, following up on the threats.'

Why are they always lurking around? I collect all the printed articles before entering the lift. When the doors open, Officer Levi and Kelly are waiting there with a sturdy white man in a brown suit.

Officer Levi sneers at Rap. 'Look who we have here.'

The police tell Lizzie's manager, aka Brown Suit, that they need to talk to us urgently about the threats to the *Folkshore Gazette* and, like an idiot, he believes their lies. We're in the conference room with no windows: we're trapped in here with them.

Officer Levi scowls at us from across the table.

'Hi, I'm Officer Kelly and this is my partner, Officer Levi. You're not under arrest. We just want to ask you a few questions.'

Is he acting like we haven't met before?

Red looks them directly in the eyes. 'I know my rights. We know who you are and we're not answering any of your questions. If we're not under arrest, then we're free to go.'

Officer Levi slams the table with his hoof, baring his long, yellow teeth at us. 'Stop messing us about! You may have pulled the wool over my sergeant's eyes, but you won't do that with me. We know it was your group who came into Folkshore that night. Which one of you is the mole? Our boss needs to know.'

Red and Rap push back from the table to stand up, but I really want to know who their boss is.

'You listen to me,' Officer Levi spits. 'You're not leaving this place until you tell us.'

Officer Kelly looks warily at his partner, placing a hoof on his arm. 'We don't mean no harm. We desperately need to know who came into Folkshore with you that night.'

'As we said before, no comment,' Red replies.

Officer Levi kicks the table, driving it into my stomach. I fall back, but Red catches me.

Rap switches. 'You police officers are all the same!'

Officer Kelly tries to de-escalate the situation, but his partner has lost it. 'Ca-calm down, Officer Levi.'

Officer Levi laughs crudely. 'Wait your turn, *Rap*. We can all be on our way if you just tell us what we need to know. You came here looking for your reporter friend. Anna, was it?'

'How do you know that?' I ask.

'It doesn't matter *how* I know,' Officer Levi says. 'If you don't want to end up like her, then I suggest you start talking. Now!' He hops over the table and charges towards us. Using all my strength, I swing my bag to connect with Officer Levi, and he staggers back. Rap kicks him in the leg and he drops to the ground with a thud.

Officer Kelly hurries across the room and tugs his partner back, restraining him. 'Officer Levi, calm down—that's enough.'

Officer Levi flares his nostrils. 'You already know what will happen if we don't get the truth out of them.'

The door handle rattles. 'Is everything okay in there? Girls?'

'Help!' I yell.

Officer Kelly releases Officer Levi, who charges again and

knocks into Red. The side of her head slams into the wall. Red moans, cupping her ear as blood trickles between her fingers.

'Get away from her!' Rap shouts and shoves Officer Levi, who loses his balance and falls to the ground.

The door handle rattles again. 'What's going on in there?'

I move around the table to get to the door, and Rap goes to help Red, but Officer Levi isn't done. His hoof clamps down on my afro and drags me to the floor. With a heaving chest, Officer Levi towers over me and uses his hoof to crush my hand.

I scream.

Officer Kelly charges at his partner for the last time.

'Get up,' Rap grunts and helps me up from the floor. 'We have to go.'

We unlock the door and stumble out into the corridor, where we bump into a distraught-looking Lizzie. 'Oh my lord! You're hurt. What happened in there?'

Chapter 17

When we arrive at the hospital, the waiting room isn't too busy so we plan what we're going to do. My swollen hand looks like puff puff, and the side of Red's face is discoloured. This is worse than when my family went to a Nigerian hall party and got food poisoning from the pepper soup served there. One toilet. Six people. How do you spell traumatised?

'When I tell people about the police, they don't like to listen,' Rap rages.

Red's iPhone goes off and Ty's picture appears on the screen.

'Don't answer it,' Rap warns.

'What do you mean? I can't just ignore it.' Red's bruised finger hovers over the green call symbol.

'You *know* that Ty will do something stupid,' Rap explains. 'You can tell him later when your face doesn't look like that.'

Red twists her mouth to the side. 'Fine.' She messages Ty and switches off her phone.

A rabbit dressed in a yellow shift dress and with pearls around her neck approaches us. 'Hello, I'm Dr Ida. What happened here, ladies?'

Rap rushes to answer. 'We were in an accident.'

Dr Ida's pager goes off several times. 'Excuse me ladies, there's an emergency, but Nurse Rose will look after you.'

Nurse Rose, a white woman with rosy cheeks, says, 'Let's get you all looked at.' She leads us through the hospital. The sterile smell clings to our clothes. It doesn't matter where you are, hospitals smell the same.

The nurse draws back a curtain to reveal a bed and two chairs. When we first came to Deji's hospital, I sat in the furthest chair away from his bed because I was worried about touching the wrong thing. He'd joked that tumours weren't contagious. He's always joking about something! I know Deji would find a way to make me laugh at this situation.

Nurse Rose pulls on her blue gloves, then gestures to Red to take a seat on the chair.

'There is some bruising and a few cuts. How is your head feeling?' she asks Red while cleaning her wound. 'Oh, Dr Eric, I didn't see you there.' Her voice has gone high and her dull brown eyes sparkle.

Dr Eric looks like a fairy-tale prince. With his parted, mahogany hair, white teeth, and height, all that's missing is a stallion to rescue princesses on.

'She luv man,' Red whispers and we laugh.

'It's just so concerning, don't you think, Dr Eric?' Nurse Rose asks. 'Death rates related to heart attacks are rising.'

Dr Eric hums, clearly not paying attention as he inspects my left hand. I wince in pain.

'We're going to need an X-ray for your hand. I don't think it's broken, but I like to be thorough.'

'How is your coma patient today?' Nurse Rose asks, attempting to conversate with him again. 'The one from Once Upon a Time Street. Is he still unresponsive?'

The man I saw being attacked by the Shrieker? Did he survive?

'Yes, he's still in a Sleeping Beauty coma.' Dr Eric coughs and blinks rapidly. 'If you follow me, we can get you sorted out with that X-ray now.' He leads me through the hospital to the Damsel Wing, where they X-ray my hand.

'It's not broken. A compression bandage should help with any swelling,' Dr Eric explains. 'You need to ice it for three to four days, and I'll prescribe you painkillers. If the swelling doesn't go down after a few days, then come back.'

Dr Eric's pager goes off as Rap and Red appear. The vein in Rap's forehead throbs, and I know something is wrong.

'We have to go now,' Rap insists. 'Ty and the others know what happened to us.'

'But how did they find out?'

'Someone at the *Folkshore Gazette* must've figured out what happened and leaked it.' Rap walks out of the hospital.

Was it Lizzie?

Westley marches across the road towards us, his face a harsh blizzard. He flips his baseball cap the other way around.

'I'm fine,' Rap bites.

'This is *insane*, Rap,' Westley exclaims, flexing his muscles.

'I had to come and see for myself. So it's true then, the police did this to you?'

Westly reaches out to touch Rap's face, but she steps away and her face hardens. 'We didn't just stand there. We fought back.'

'I didn't mean...' He clears his throat. 'Everyone is here for you—for all three of you.'

A large group of protestors walk down the street with Ty leading them. They are shouting and screaming.

'Red!' Ty yells.

The crowd surrounds us, inspecting our injuries, which fuels more hate. The police pigs trot forward. Westley right by her side, Rap stands in front of them, Docs to hooves.

'Protect, not neglect!' Rap screams.

'Protect, not neglect!' the crowd repeats. 'Protect, not neglect! Protect, not neglect!'

A glass bottle flies past me, narrowly missing my face. As I pivot, I collide with Prince. We get tossed further into the crowd. One of the police pigs wrestles with a young woman and they both collapse to the ground. Cans crash against the ground and release smoke that burns our eyes. We scatter like ants.

Chapter 18

People wander around Prince and me in the packed common room all morning, commenting on what happened yesterday, like, 'I can't believe that happened to you, Leah', 'The police are wrong to do that.' The worst one was from Mal: 'I'm going to do everything in my power to make sure those officers pay.'

But all this is happening because the police were looking for me! If I turn myself in, will it make everything better? Maybe then the police boss will stop looking for me.

I add to the small pile of revision cards we've made. Police or no police, I promised Prince that we would study, and I don't want to fall behind.

'Ya can't keep blamin' yourself for what the pigs did to ya.' Prince runs his hands through his long hair. 'Everything's gone arseways, but things were mental before you came.'

Bran pulls out a chair at the table and sits down. 'You should've called me. I would've shown 'em what for.'

'We didn't need you to save us, Bran,' I reply. 'They shouldn't have attacked us in the first place.'

'What's that prick doing on TV?' Ty calls out.

Cameras flash, reflecting off Edward's practised gaze. 'What transpired last night on the streets of Folkshore was completely unacceptable, and the Assembly condemns it. Keeping people safe is the first duty of this council. We are shocked by the astonishing acts of violence towards the police. Police officers have been assaulted, and innocent people caught in the crossfire. We will not stand for this violation and separation from order. Investigations will commence soon into those we believe are involved in this barbaric movement against Folkshore. We must ensure that nothing like this happens again, and protect the citizens of Folkshore from these criminals.'

So it's acceptable for the police to attack and lie to people, but we can't stand up for ourselves?

'This is rubbish!'

'Let them come then!'

'Nahhhhh.'

Mal claps her ring-clad hands together to get everyone's attention, and the room quietens instantly. 'What happened last night was atrocious, and I'll be speaking to the police commissioner this morning. Until then, please can everyone stay safe? The police want us to slip up. I'll be calling for a board of directors meeting to make sure we're covered.'

The camera changes to Rumpelstiltskin, who is being quizzed about the protests too. 'I'm sickened by the excessive violence shown by the police yesterday and the hurt experienced by the Folkshorian community. I stand by the community today at this abuse of power from two of their very own.'

Prince's phone vibrates and he shows me the message.

Rap

> Meeting at the community centre

> Bring Fola with you

'I'm coming too,' Bran says, standing up. 'You're not leaving me out again.'

Red meets us at the entrance of the community centre, then leads us through the building and downstairs. There's a glowing light coming from the room right at the end, which must be full of people. I can hear lots of voices.

The room reminds me of an underground den in an action movie, where the main characters plot how they're going to defeat the bad guy. Pascal, Westley, Ty, Cindy and some other Folkshorians sit on mismatched chairs around a table in the centre of a well-lit room.

Cindy envelops me in a hug before I have the chance to find a seat. 'Oh, sweetie. How is your hand?'

'It's better, thanks. The swelling has gone down.'

'Everyone's here now,' Rap says, standing at the head

of the table. 'Some of you already know what happened to us yesterday, but there's more.' She tells them about what I recorded, the documentary idea and Leonard's shop. Anger seeps into the room until you can almost taste it.

'The police and the Assembly are supposed to be here to protect us, but they're against us, so we have to protect ourselves,' Rap says.

'What else did you find out from the *Gazette*?' Pascal asks, coughing into his handkerchief. 'Anything we can use against them?' Pascal's fur looks drier and more matted than when I saw him last. I can't be the only one who's noticed. And it *can't* just be the air causing it.

'Yeah,' I reply, pulling the papers out of my bag. 'We found some interesting articles.'

Red holds up the report she printed. 'I think this is the report that Tabitha was talking about in Leah's recording.'

'Give it here. I bet I can work it out. Sherlock and Wottie on the case.' Bran snatches the paper out of Red's hand. 'An investigation into the spectral phenomena of Folkshore—'

Red snatches the paper back. 'Don't snatch things out of my hand. You ask.'

Bran sticks out her tongue in response because she is literally five years old. 'Spectral is somethin' to do with spectacles so it's about glasses,' Bran guesses. 'Obviously, the Assembly can't read.'

Pascal leans forward, inspecting the report closely. 'A similar word to spectral is otherworldly. Can I take a look at it, please?'

'Yes, you may, because you asked politely,' Red replies sweetly and looks pointedly at Bran. 'Yuh nuh hav nuh mannaz.'

'Fascinating.' Pascal strokes his grey, furry chin and addresses the room. 'From what I can decipher, it is an investigation into Folkshore's ecosystem. I wonder why the previous Assembly was looking into that. Curious. Well, whatever type of investigation it is, this is only the introduction.' He points to a number at the bottom. 'I recognise this reference number right here. The full report should be filed in the town hall's Albany Room, which is in the restricted section. Only privileged people, such as Assembly members, can use their ID cards to access that room.'

'Why don't you just nick the ID card off your dad, Cindy?' Bran blurts out.

Cindy shifts uncomfortably in her seat. 'I can't do that, but I'll see what I can do... if I can talk to him.'

'I have an idea,' I say. 'Before the documentary is ready, why don't we start posting videos online about whatever we find?'

'I can set up an account,' Red says.

'Yeah,' Westley agrees. 'Knowledge is power.'

I can't keep lying to everyone about who I am and why the police are after a mole.

Clearing my throat, I go through the long speech in my head. 'I'm not from here.' As I speak, the room quietens down and everyone looks at me. 'My name isn't Leah and I'm *not* Red's cousin. My name is Fola, and I'm from Kent. I came into Folkshore by accident. I'm not supposed to be here. I've been trying to get home to my brother. Now the police are looking for me, and I don't know why.' I let out a long breath.

Cindy nods, as if she's processing every bit of information. 'I *knew* it! I knew there was something up. Fola, you're a *terrible* liar.'

A few people in the room laugh and agree. Why are they agreeing so quickly, though? I'm not *that* bad at lying.

'I've already told ya about your thinking out loud problem, Fols.' Prince chuckles.

Ty does a double take. 'I didn't know. I thought you were actually Red's cousin. Why are the feds looking for you, though?'

I shrug. 'I dunno, but they can't hear you lot calling me Fola because they know the beginning of my name.'

'Let's get back to business.' Rap knocks the table, drawing everyone's attention back to her. 'We need to talk about what we're going to do about these new restrictions the Assembly have announced...'

Once we're done with the meeting, everyone gets ready to leave, but I catch Pascal before he goes. I want to show him the article I found about the auction of the mysterious tablet.

'How intriguing,' Pascal says, looking at the article.

'Why would Rumpelstiltskin bid that much for it?' I ask. 'No one knows what's in it.'

'Well, it *is* something of a rare commodity, and I know that Rumpelstiltskin is an avid collector. But we've got a mystery on our hands. How did the tablet end up in a private auction in the first place? Can I hold on to this? I would love to reach out to a few of my contacts.'

Bran, who I didn't know was listening, asks, 'If you want to know, why don't you just go and speak to Rumpelstiltskin yourself? The last time we saw the fella he said, "my door is always open," or whatever.'

'We can't just show up at his house.' *Fola, you followed a group of random people into a hidden mythical place, but you can't go and ask one man a few questions?* I berate myself. 'Okay, but I don't wanna go alone. Do you know where Rumpelstiltskin lives?'

'Nah, but I bet the fitty lives in some kinda mansion.'

Tugging on his black beanie, Prince says, 'Rumpelstiltskin Gold. I know where he lives. Why'd you wanna know?'

Chapter 19

'I fucking knew it!' Bran exclaims as we stand outside Rumpel's mini castle.

White stone statues are artistically arranged around a golden fountain which shoots crystal-blue water into the air, which contrasts with the off-white colour of the mansion. This place is massive.

We climb a set of steps to a wide wooden door with one of those brass lion's-head knockers.

'Rumpel's a private investor,' Prince says. 'A couple of the fellas from Greenwood are training with him to get started.'

The front door creaks open, and we come face to face with Rumpel, who's wearing a pressed white shirt and brown chinos.

'Ah, Prince, Branna, Leah. How can I help you? Did we have an appointment scheduled today?'

The other two wait for me to speak. I didn't tell them the whole reason I wanted to speak to Rumpel. They think it's for the secret investigation we're doing into the Assembly.

'We wanted to ask you some questions about the community work you do,' I answer.

'Inquisitive minds bite the head of the lion many a time.'

'You what?' Bran whispers. 'You're always confusing me.'

Prince snorts.

'Come in. Unfortunately, this will have to be brief as I have a meeting shortly. I'll do my best to answer any questions you may have.'

If we thought the outside was impressive, the inside is even better, with its white spiral staircase and golden chandeliers. The hardwood floors are so polished that I swear I can see myself in them. It's another St Joseph's.

We pass a wall full of artwork that looks like it costs more money than I've ever seen. At first, I think it's my eyes playing tricks, but the wall is moving like a wave.

Beside me, Prince whistles and points to an abstract piece. 'It's an original Kandinsky,' he says in amazement.

'What's a Kandinsky?' Bran asks. 'All I see are some shapes and boxes. They sell something similar in Ikea.'

Rumpelstiltskin clasps Prince's shoulder. His gold signet ring gleams. 'A man with taste and a good eye. I acquired it at a private auction in Vienna.'

'Must've cost you heaps of money,' Prince replies.

'Ah, yes, but you can't put a price on art. Why don't we sit down, and you can ask me all the questions you want?'

I sink into a vintage, backless lounge chair with a curved armrest. I prop myself up, so I don't fall backwards and embarrass myself. 'What kind of things do you collect?'

'I collect all sorts of items, as you can see.' Rumpel gestures around the room. 'I like to collect the finest of the finest, the top echelon of antiques, from paintings to rare books and clocks.'

'I saw in the newspaper about a private auction for a tablet about a year ago. *The Chronicles of Folkshore.*' I sound casual, but I'm sweating.

Rumpel crosses his legs and readjusts himself in his seat. 'Ah, yes, *The Chronicles of Folkshore.* I was taken by its rarity, history and value. However, it was stolen a few months ago, and the police never caught the perpetrator. Do you have any other questions for me?'

'Yeah, I do,' Bran butts in before I can ask Rumpel anything else about the tablet. 'You're a pretty decent bloke. Why do you work with the Assembly? They're basically screwing over the people in this community with all their new plans.'

Rumpel spreads his hands like a politician would. 'Most of our dealings are about my work with the community and other areas. I'm not privy to *all* their plans, only some.' He checks his rose-gold watch for the second time.

'You seemed pretty bloody *privy* in that secret town hall—'

'Exhibition,' Prince blurts out, covering Bran's slip-up. 'Is that an Alberti limited edition watch?'

Rumpel beats the face of his watch and replies, 'It is— good man. We will have to wrap this up now. I have a call with the Assembly's site managers for an update about Folkshore station.'

All the breath is bottled up in my chest at the idea that

Folkshore station could be finished. I need to go home to see Deji and my family. 'Have they finished?'

'Not quite. The reports the Assembly provided me with show the storm did considerable damage internally.'

How can he believe the Assembly without asking any questions? They could be spending all the money and lying about it.

A notification for a meeting appears on Rumpel's phone and he ushers us out of his house, saying that we can come back any time.

As soon as the door shuts behind us, I say, 'If the Assembly have been lying about everything else, what's to say they're not lying about the station too?'

'Good detective work, Wottie.' Bran hums.

'If you're right, we can get proof for the doc,' Prince agrees. 'I know a shortcut to the station.'

Scaffolding and plastic tarp cover the station, shielding the construction work going on inside. We look through the hazy purple glass. An armed guard with tense shoulders and dark sunglasses patrols the station.

'Oi! Where are you going?' Bran asks.

I duck under the scaffolding. The automatic doors open, and I step inside. My mouth hangs open, because it's like I thought. The station has been fixed inside. I take out my camera and snap a few pictures of the fully refurbished station.

'You were right!' Bran shouts. 'Those twats were lying.'

We don't realise until it's too late that the armed guard has called for backup.

'You three shouldn't be in here,' she sneers, her hand inching towards her weapon.

As the two armed guards close in on us, we scatter. All the pods in the station are made of glass except one small kiosk. I grab the handle and find that it's unlocked, thank God. I squeeze myself under the counter, praying they don't find me—or the others.

'Get the fuck off me!' Bran shouts.

Heavy footsteps thunder towards where I'm hiding, and I think I've been caught, but they run past me.

'I caught the other one,' the first guard says. 'Take them underground.'

Chapter 20

I follow them through the security door and down the stairs, leading into the tunnels. I hear them talking through the gap under the first metal door. Pacing outside, half of me is thinking about what the guards could be doing to my friends and the other half is thinking that I got myself into another mess.

Both guards step out of the room to take a call, locking the room behind them. I dive around the corner, catching my shoulder on the wall.

'Hello, boss,' the first guard answers.

Who is this boss?

'It was a false alarm,' the guard says. 'We found some kids lurking around the station. I think they're the same ones as... yes... yes, boss.' The guard's shoulders tighten and his hand trembles at his boss's words. 'No, I'm sorry, boss. I understand completely and I promise that it won't happen again.'

He passes the phone to the second guard, who takes it reluctantly. The guards are outside the room—this could be my chance to get my friends out. I slip back up the stairs and smash the glass of the fire alarm by the security door and pull down the handle. I hide so they don't see me. The fire alarm wails, flooding the station with noise and alerting the guards, who bolt up the stairs and out the door. I run back down and grab the handle of the door to the room where Bran and Prince are being kept. The doorknob shakes and rotates, but it's locked.

'Don't you have like a hammer or something like that?' Bran says from the other side of the door.

'Why would she be carrying around a hammer?' Prince asks Bran, as confused as I am. 'Ya see anything else you can use?'

Looking around, I spot the fire extinguisher attached to the wall. 'Found something.'

I grab the fire extinguisher and smash it against the door.

'Hit it again!' Bran yells.

The squealing of the fire alarms stops, which means the guards will be back down here any minute. Swinging the extinguisher above my head, I hit the doorknob with all my strength, and it breaks. My friends run out through the broken door.

'We have to go—now. I know the way.' I've studied those blueprints like they were one of my exams. We journey deeper into the tunnels and it grows darker. If I'm right, we should come out at the manhole cover on the street by the junction.

Holding on to the wall, Bran asks, 'Fols, you sure this is the way out? We've been walking for *ages* and all these tunnels look the bloody same.'

'Eustace gave you something, didn't he?' Prince whispers bitterly. His icy eyes penetrate mine like daggers. 'The last time we were down here, ya didn't know your arse from your elbow.'

'Eustace gave me the blueprints, but I wasn't supposed to tell anyone.'

'But you wouldn't have gotten those blueprints without me. Ya know I want to get out of Folkshore too.'

Noah. Of course. But how could Prince think I wouldn't tell him if I knew a way out?

I lower my voice in case Bran is listening. 'I swear I'll tell you if I find anything. I know you want to get back to Noah, and I want to get back to my brother. I wouldn't keep that from you.'

Prince nods, running his hand through his hair.

'Lovers' tiff, eh?' Bran says, and we separate. 'That's why I can't do love and all that business. It's not for me.'

I rub my eyes and point ahead of us. 'The exit should be down there.'

There's a shrill shriek. My stomach roils in fear. The vision comes suddenly. My eyes adjust to the darkness around me, and I realise that I'm in the corner of a peach-coloured cage in a circular room and a large water tank in the centre. A dozen Shriekers are huddled in the corner of the cage. A familiar fear chills my body.

Then I'm back in the tunnel with Bran and Prince.

'Please. Help me,' a shaky voice cries from behind us.

An older black man with thin grey hair and a scraggly beard staggers towards us in soiled clothes.

'Leonard?' Prince asks, confused. 'Where have ya been? We thought you... We didn't know what happened to ya.'

This can't be the same man Cindy was talking about. He stumbles, but Prince catches his fragile body before it hits the ground.

'Thank you, son,' he rasps, coughing into a dusty handkerchief. 'I didn't leave. They wouldn't let me leave.'

'Why not?' Prince asks.

'Because I knew what they're doing to Folkshore. I... need to get outside. I need air.'

I don't realise I'm standing there, staring at him, until Bran's shoulder brushes mine. 'Wottie, we need to get out of here.'

'It's this way.'

Leonard leans on Prince for support as we move towards the exit, and our freedom. Finally, we reach the steps up to the manhole by the junction. Leonard stumbles ahead, grabbing the railing like a lifeline, and begins to climb up.

'Make sure you check for traffic,' I say.

Slowly, Bran pushes at the manhole cover to open it, checking for cars on the road. 'All clear.'

She opens it fully, and we climb out into more darkness.

'Finally!' Bran shouts.

Moving Leonard to the side of the junction, a huge lorry speeds over the dented manhole, making a sound like a train on tracks. Leonard takes a deep breath in the humid air before dropping to the ground and kissing it. 'Thank God I found you kids.'

'Leonard,' Prince says softly. 'Who kept you down there?'

Fat tears stream down Leonard's face, mixing with the dirt. 'I-I can't talk about it. He will know. Please.'

Prince's eyes flash with anger. 'Who is he?'

Leonard curls into himself. 'No. No. No. I've already said too much. He knows everything... he knows... I-I can't.'

'Bloody 'ell,' Bran whispers.

Holding Leonard tightly around the waist, Prince helps him to a bench. 'Leonard, there has to be some way we can help ya. Jesus. Someone kept you down there.'

'Were you the only one down there?' I ask, thinking about all the others the Assembly supposedly said left Folkshore. 'We should take you to a hospital to be checked.'

'No. There were others. I need to get away from here. I can't talk about it now.' He gets up and begins to walk away. 'No hospitals.'

'Leonard, wait. Let me take ya home,' Prince bellows after him, but Leonard doesn't stop. He hobbles across the road, almost getting hit by a car.

We keep off the main streets and head back to Greenwood. No one says a word for a while.

'We can tell Mal in the morning,' Bran murmurs. 'She always knows what to do.'

'I just can't believe it,' Prince replies.

I can't believe it either.

We say goodnight, but I don't know if any of us will be able to sleep. As I drop my bag on the floor in my room, there's a blood-curdling shriek. A shadowy form is outside the window. I leave my door wide open, running back down the corridor and out of Greenwood.

Did the Shrieker come for me?

I sneak looks over my shoulder as I rush down the high street and ring Cindy's doorbell.

Why isn't anyone answering?

I ring again.

'Who is it?' Cindy asks from behind the door, sleep heavy in her voice.

'It's me, Fola. Please, let me in... those demonic creatures are after me.'

Chapter 21

'Shhh, Mum said we shouldn't disturb her.'

'But my favourite show is on,' Maya moans, 'and I can't watch it because *she's* in the way.'

Soft, strawberry-scented curls tickle my face, making me peel my eyes open. I groan as I shift on the comfortable fabric sofa, reminding me how sore my body is.

Dani grins down at me. She has jam smeared around her mouth. 'You want some?'

She offers me a half-eaten piece of toast.

'Are you awake now?' Maya asks, hovering over me. 'My show is on.'

Cindy appears in the doorway, her lips pressed tightly together. 'What did I tell you, Maya?'

Munching her peanut-buttered toast, Maya shrugs, picking up the remote. 'You said we couldn't disturb her because she was sleeping, but she's *not* sleeping anymore.'

'Oh really?' Cindy replies sarcastically. 'I didn't notice. If you don't behave, no TV for you.'

Maya pouts, sticking out her bottom lip. 'Sorry, Mum.'

In her black Batman onesie and with her curly hair in pigtails, Maya looks adorable, but we all know the truth, including her mum.

'Maya, that's not going to work on me.' Cindy wags her finger. 'And make sure your sister gets a turn too. I don't want to hear anything about you charging your little sister money to watch her programmes. Do you understand me?'

'Yes, Muuuuum,' Maya grumbles.

I hide a smile at her scamming ways.

'Would you like some breakfast, sweetie?' Cindy's strict demeanour flips to a cheery one. 'I can make you something. What about some pancakes?'

At the mention of pancakes, I swing my legs off the sofa, get up, and follow Cindy into the kitchen. She whizzes around as I pour myself a cup of freshly brewed tea and take a sip, waking myself up. With the clear bowl resting on her right hip, Cindy whisks the pancake batter. 'Sweetie, what happened to you last night?'

My head throbs. Yesterday was mad. From Bran and Prince getting arrested, to my vision, to Leonard, then to the creature outside my window. Why is Folkshore like this? What's happening?

Cindy uses a ladle to scoop batter into the frying pan on the cooker then turns, leaning against the countertop. 'You were saying something about demonic creatures from hell?'

If I tell everyone Shriekers are real and I'm seeing these visions, will they think I'm one of those fake psychics?

'What do you know about Shriekers?' I ask.

'What do I know about Shriekers?' Cindy says slowly. 'I haven't heard about them for years now. When I was growing up, there were these myths about them. They were reputed to be people who were so evil, they changed into those dark creatures. Shriekers.'

So, Red said they're evil creatures who eat children and now Cindy is saying that evil people turned into Shriekers, but my last vision makes me think that someone is controlling them. Why were they trapped inside that cage?

'Why do you ask?'

Ding dong.

'Can you watch the pancakes, please?' Cindy asks, leaving the kitchen to answer the door.

There's a pounding on the stairs, loud voices, and then Bran barges through the living room into the kitchen, followed by the rest of the group. The kitchen is packed. I switch off the gas, looking sadly at my failed breakfast. Turning around, I find everyone staring at me like I'm on the stand in court.

'Why are you all looking at me like that?' I ask, crossing my arms.

Bran chews on her gum so aggressively, I'm scared she's going to bite her tongue off. 'Are you having a laugh? One minute you were in Greenwood and then you'd bloody disappeared—even Mal is worried about you. We called *them* asking if they knew where you were.' She points to Rap and Red.

While Red is observing me like I'm a victim in one of her law shows, Rap has her usual annoyed expression on her face.

Prince leans on the door post. 'What happened to ya after the tunnels, lass?'

Red frowns, confused. 'Wait—why were you in the tunnels?'

I scratch the back of my neck and clear my throat nervously. 'So, Bran and Prince kind of got arrested at the station because of me.'

'Arrested!' Cindy cries.

'Of course you got yourselves arrested,' Rap taunts, rolling her eyes.

'We didn't do it on bloody purpose, did we?' Bran bellows, popping her gum.

Rap shoots angry glances at us. 'What were you even doing at the station? Isn't it closed?'

I explain everything that happened yesterday, excluding all the questions I asked Rumpel, the vision, and me knowing the layout of the tunnels, because they don't need to know all that.

'You found Leonard.' Cindy covers her mouth, the tears pooling into her cupped palm. 'Oh no.' She sniffs. 'Poor Leonard.'

'I *knew* it,' Rap rages, stamping her foot. 'All those missing people. I *knew* something was wrong.'

'Sweetie, we don't know the full story yet.' Cindy tries to comfort Rap, but she's not listening; she's already on her phone shouting about it to Westley.

'Nah, that means there's a *kidnapper* in Folkshore,' Red

says. 'We're not safe.' Her phone beeps five times, and she glances at it. 'Guys, Leonard is trending.'

'How?' Prince asks, scrunching up his face. 'How'd they know?'

Red flips her phone around to show us a picture on Flitter of Leonard looking haggard, roaming the streets. He's wearing the same clothes as yesterday. Someone must've seen him. The shares and likes are in the thousands, and they're still rising.

'And you should see all the comments under your video of Leonard's shop,' Red continues. 'Watch when we post about what Leonard told you—the Assembly won't be able to stay quiet.'

'I don't think Leonard wants us to tell everyone what happened to him. It's bad enough that his picture is plastered everywhere,' Prince growls. 'You should've seen him yesterday. He was shaking like a leaf. I had to basically hold him up.'

'But people need to know what's happening.' Red frowns, tilting her head to one side. 'It's *kidnapping*. We don't even know who took him or why they took him. Wouldn't you want to know?'

Red is right. People *do* need to know what's going on, but this is much bigger than I expected it to be. I thought we could expose the Assembly while I figured out a way out of here.

'I'm going to see him,' Cindy announces, wiping her face and putting on her wool princess coat. 'I've known him all my life. He was like a father to me when my own father wasn't. We can't pressure him, especially...' She hiccups. 'Especially with all the unspeakable things he's probably endured.'

'We should tell people to stay away from the tunnels,' Red says. 'I don't want to be kidnapped too.'

Ding dong.

Rap answers the door this time, and reappears with Westley. While Rap fills him in, Cindy gets ready to go to Leonard's house to see him. I decide to go with her in case he agrees to me interviewing him.

'I'm going into the tunnels,' Rap says as Westley attempts to speak. 'Don't try and talk me out of it, Westley. We've been out on the streets for months! We knew it.' She slaps the back of her hand into her palm. 'We have to go down there.'

The same tunnels that the Shriekers might live in? No way am I going back down there.

Westley puts his hands on Rap's shoulders, stopping her pacing. 'Rap, I'm not trying to stop you. I'm agreeing with you, okay? If we can get enough people together, we can go down there. You don't have to go alone.'

'I've messaged Anastasia already to come and look after the girls. I'm leaving the house key here for the rest of you.' Cindy places a key on the table. 'I'm ready to go if you are.'

As we step out onto the high street, heavy torrential rain beats us. The only thing I can make out are the luminous trees.

'This weather,' Cindy complains, forcing open her see-through umbrella. 'I'm really worried about Leonard,' she whispers. 'He did so much for the community, and it feels like the same community failed him... like *I* failed him.'

How can Cindy think that?

'You didn't know someone was gonna kidnap him, though.'

After a few seconds, the rain suddenly stops and the sun reappears in the clear blue sky, roasting us as if it wasn't just raining. Cindy closes her umbrella and shakes out the excess water.

'I was 19 when I left Folkshore for Paris with my boyfriend Michael, who would become my husband,' Cindy explains. 'My mum left my father once I'd gone, and he thought the whole world had abandoned him. I'm the youngest of three. My own father shut me out and wouldn't talk to me for years because I left—as if what I did was bad enough for him not to want to see his granddaughters. When he found out Michael had died, do you know what he said?'

'What?' I ask, knowing it's going to be bad.

'My father said that maybe now I'd know what it feels like to be abandoned. Leonard was there for *years* as a father to me when my father wasn't. We have to find a way to help him.'

Leonard's cottage is the last lilac one on Beanstalk Lane.

'Here we go.' Cindy rings the bell.

The curtains shift and Leonard shouts from inside. 'Go away! I don't want to talk to anyone.'

Cindy sticks her hand through the letterbox and speaks through it. 'Leonard, it's me, Cindy. I just want to talk to you. I just want to know that you're okay.'

'Cinderella, is that really you?' There's movement in the house and the grey door unlocks to reveal Leonard's worn face. 'Come inside before anyone sees you.'

Cindy scoops him into a hug. 'I knew you wouldn't leave without telling me.' She inhales. 'I'm so sorry this happened to you.'

Leonard's bony hand pats Cindy's back feebly as he replies, 'I know, Cinderella. I know.'

A thick layer of dust coats Leonard's aged wooden furniture like an extra layer of skin. He clears a chair of old newspapers and letters that have piled up since he's been away. 'I didn't know... anyone was coming today.'

'Leonard, it's fine. You don't need to clear up for us.' Gently, Cindy takes the papers from him. 'Please, sit down and rest. You need it.'

A black and brown striped cat with yellow eyes creeps out from under the chair, rubbing itself against Leonard's leg.

'Since when did you have a cat?' Cindy asks.

Picking the cat up, Leonard places her in his lap. 'She's a stray that I found.' He strokes the cat and puts her back on the floor. 'I know you've probably come here to talk about what happened, but I'm not ready, and I don't think I'll ever be. I can't talk about it because he'll know. He always knows.'

'Who is he?' I question him. 'Can you at least tell us if any of the missing people were down there with you?'

'Yes,' he whispers. 'But I don't remember where. I don't know the tunnels.'

We have to find them.

'Leonard,' Cindy starts, but her phone beeps. 'It's the Assembly. They're holding a press conference at the town hall.'

The live stream on Cindy's phone shows a small crowd holding up photos of their missing family members.

Lizzie reports, 'We're live from the town hall, where a crowd has gathered to demand answers from the Assembly. Pictures have circulated online of Leonard James, a pillar of the community, who many believed had left Folkshore approximately six months ago after taking the money offered to him by the Assembly. However, there are now rumours of a possible kidnapping ring in Folkshore. Leonard has yet to provide a statement on his whereabouts over the past six months.'

The crowd stirs as Roland emerges from the town hall and approaches the podium. 'Fellow Folkshorians, the Assembly were sickened to hear about a possible kidnapping ring in Folkshore. In order for us to keep everyone safe, the Assembly has issued a curfew of 4pm for all Folkshorians, effective immediately, until we have apprehended those responsible for this heinous crime. We have put together a special taskforce to search the tunnels for any other victims. Currently, we have one person of interest. A warrant has been issued for the arrest of 17-year-old Westley Lavaly.'

Chapter 22

After Roland's statement, things go from bad to worse, as the curfew makes it difficult for us to meet on the streets. We're in Cindy's kitchen planning what to do next.

I hold on to Cindy's laptop, protecting my video edits as Rap rocks the table, scrambling for her ringing phone. 'Mal! Have you spoken to Westley? They need to release him.'

Red whispers to Rap, 'Tell Mal that, legally, they can't keep him locked up without any evidence.'

Rap pulls the phone away from her ear to respond. 'Apparently, they're saying that they have *substantial* evidence that he is part of this kidnapping ring. Westley. Human trafficking. They're the sick ones, not him!' Slamming the phone on the table, Rap grunts in frustration. 'I can't believe this. Leonard even told them that Westley wasn't involved. We have to do something.'

Cindy settles her cup back on the plate. 'Rapunzel, you're right. We do have to do something. I'm going to call my father again for any news on Westley. Maybe their special taskforce can help us look in the tunnels.'

The only person Roland cares about is Roland. Everyone

knows if something is going to happen, it won't be because of his help.

'And wait for Roland to do what?' Red asks, kissing her teeth. 'Our page has, like, 100k followers already and it's doing more for Folkshore than the Assembly are doing. Watch when the documentary is released. I have more people that you need to interview.'

Pausing the video on the laptop, I ask Red, 'Who else is on the list?'

'Gran and Auntie Pauline are getting their hair ready for their interviews, and I told them I'd do their make-up.'

'It's not a bloody photo shoot,' Bran moans as her phone rings. 'Pas. What's wrong? Oh, yeah. I've already told her about the film equipment. Yeah, she's here.' Bran hands me her phone. 'Pas wants to speak to you.'

'Hi, Pascal.'

'Hi. I did some digging and discovered something very interesting about our special tablet. When you pick up the film equipment, I can tell you all about it.'

'Okay, see you later.'

I drop Bran's phone and move to sit on Cindy's sofa. Prince is sketching a young boy as a superhero, with his cape holding up a building.

'Who is that?' I ask, distracting myself.

'Noah—my brother. I'll give it to him if I ever get to see him again.' Prince tears the drawing out of his sketchbook and tucks it into the back of the sketchbook with the rest of his finished pieces.

'How'd you get so good at drawing?'

Prince starts to sketch the outline of a new piece. 'I had to find something to keep my baby brothers busy, so I started sketching these little comics. Noah always begged me to do them. I could say the same thing about your photographs. They're something fierce.'

I try to hide my smile.

'You better get it, Fola!' Red shouts from across the room, laughing.

One thing that Bran and Red agree on is teasing me about Prince, even though there's nothing going on. They're so embarrassing.

'I didn't mean to embarrass you or anythin'.' Prince chuckles.

Cindy mumbles in frustration. 'My father's still not answering my calls after that sorry excuse of a press conference. It's so typical of him not to be there when I need him.'

'I'm not tryna be rude or nothing, Cindy,' Bran starts, her voice muffled by her third slice of chocolate cake. 'But your dad's a bit of a dickhead.'

Cindy nods. 'You know what, Branna, I think you're right. We're going to have to do it all ourselves. We have enough people willing to help.'

'Ty said there are people waiting at the tunnel's entrance already,' Red replies, checking her phone. 'Fola, are sure you know the tunnels? Cos I don't wanna get trapped down there.'

'Yeah, and Prince drew me these.' On the kitchen table, I stack a small pile of hand-drawn maps of the tunnels near where Leonard was. I'm just praying that we don't see any Shriekers—maybe they'll leave us alone.

Cindy places a bundle of Maya's glow-in-the-dark stickers on the table. 'Maya made me promise that I wouldn't take the best ones. Now, let's go and find those people.'

Leaving Cindy's flat, we keep to the side streets, so the police don't see us. The chilling cold is Folkshore's new norm; dark clouds perch on top of the twisted trees.

Rap addresses the crowd of people at the entrance to the tunnels. 'Thanks for showing up. We're going to split into two groups, but make sure you mark the walls with these stickers, so you don't get lost—and use the maps we're going to hand out.'

We descend into the dark tunnel using our phone torches to guide us. I swallow my nerves. I can't believe I'm down here again.

'Bran, why did you wear those?' I point to her heeled boots. 'Your feet are going to hurt.'

After five minutes, Bran starts complaining. I ignore her.

'Eediat,' Red cusses.

Bran stops, turning back with narrowed eyes. 'What did you just call me?'

Cindy wipes the sweat off her brow. 'Come on now, ladies. We're here to help, not start arguments.'

A squeal and a bang ricochet down the tunnel.

'Nah, did you hear that?' Red asks, waving her phone around, blinding us.

'It was nothing.' Ty hugs Red from behind to comfort her.

'None of them can try to sneak up on us anyways.' Ty darts from left to right like a boxer, jabbing his fists in the air.

Another sound echoes down the tunnel. It's closer than the first.

'Ahhh! It's a rat!' Red yells, jumping onto Ty's back. The rat leaps off the tunnel walls and scurries past into the darkness.

'See, honey,' Cindy says softly. 'It was just a rat.'

'They're coming!' one of the volunteers screams from behind us. I jump.

She's followed by another volunteer around our age. His leg is scraped and bleeding, and he's limping. Haunting shrieks pierce the air. My skin chills and my heart thunders in my chest. The Shriekers are coming!

'Run!' I shout.

As we dash down the dark, damp tunnel, our feet splash in puddles and we stumble. It seems like the Shriekers are getting closer. The boy with the injured leg trips, but Ty catches him.

A stitch shoots through my side. 'We're almost... at the exit.'

But it's too late.

A Shrieker appears in front of us, carrying the same metal device I saw when the earthquake happened. Tilting its head back, it shrieks, summoning another Shrieker, who emerges behind us, trapping us. Their solid white eye sockets track us, no longer misty.

'What the fuck are these things?' Ty asks, trying to sound tough, but the quiver in his voice betrays him.

The sound of my heartbeat hammering in my ears is only the reason I know I'm still alive. 'They're Shriekers. They're real.'

'My grandma was right,' Red cries, digging her fingernails into Ty's arm. 'I'm not going out like this.'

Think, Fola. How can we stop them?

My phone!

When I was in Once Upon a Time Street, my ringing phone affected the Shrieker.

If the blueprints are accurate, there should be a room behind this wall. 'When I say *now*, Bran and Red, play any ringtone on your phone,' I murmur out of the corner of my mouth. 'We need to find the way in. *Now*!'

The Shriekers glide towards us, but the loud ringtones stop them in their tracks, causing them to shriek in pain as spirals of black smoke crawls out of their mouths.

While the Shriekers cower on the floor, I feel against the tunnel wall, looking for the way in. 'I know there's a hidden door here somewhere.'

'Where is it then?' Rap shouts, joining me to tap along the wall and the rest of the group copies us.

The Shriekers fight against the sounds. One lifts up a shadowy claw, swiping at Bran.

'Oi, watch it, you bastard! Bran yells and steps back. 'Hurry, Fola! I dunno how long we can hold them.'

That's it. 'Everyone push on the wall!'

We use all our strength to push the wall behind us.

'Push harder!' Rap yells.

Slowly, the hidden door pivots open, sending us flying through the gap it creates. Bran and Red rush in through the gap too with the Shriekers attempting to follow, but we push the door closed, trapping them in the tunnels.

That was *too* close.

Right in the centre of the round room is a massive, rusted water tank with pipes connected to it from the ceiling.

Around the sides of the room are rusty steel cages with peeling peach-coloured paint. It's the room from my vision! It even has the same hospital beds with the restraints on them. Was this where Leonard was kept?

'I think they've been keeping people in here,' Red says, holding up a broken pair of glasses from a container full of discarded clothes and shoes.

'Where are they now?' I ask myself.

'You knew those creatures would be in the tunnels, didn't you?' Rap says.

'I swear... I—'

'Didn't you!' she shouts in my face.

'Rap, honey, please calm down,' Cindy says. 'If Fola knew, she would've warned us, right?'

Everyone turns to me, the guilt painted plainly on my face.

'What the actual fuck, Wottie?' Bran exclaims.

'If I told you Shriekers were real, you would've thought I was mad,' I reply.

The pipes groan above us and the water tank leaks white light. The same white light I've seen all over Folkshore.

'There's more,' I whisper and Rap glares at me.

Red crosses her arms. 'Nah, more what?'

'Oh for fuck's sake, don't tell me there are more demonic creatures!' Bran shouts.

'I think that report Tabitha was talking about is actually real.'

'About Folkshorians controlling Folkshore and there being "white light" in our blood.' Rap laughs scornfully. 'Be for real.'

'Listen, okay? I think the light is being taken from Folkshore. The night of the earthquake—that's when I first saw a Shrieker. And it had the same device in its hand. It was extracting white light from a man's chest and then that *same* man went into a Sleeping Beauty coma,' I explain, desperation leaking through my voice. 'And... and the trees are losing their white light! The light is going out in the lampposts and there's white light in there.'

I point to the water tank.

'Where do the pipes lead?' Prince asks, looking up.

'If I'm right, we're directly under the Hometree. The white light must be coming from it.'

No one says anything. *Have I lost them?*

'Someone is taking it,' I whisper.

'Is that why you were quiet the day after the earthquake?' Red asks after a while. 'Because you saw a Shrieker. Bran said it was because you broke up with Prince.'

'Priceless.' Prince chuckles.

'Bran!' I shout. Ear-piercing shrieks sound from outside the hidden door. 'More Shriekers.' They claw at the wall from outside. 'Look, I know you don't believe me yet, but you all need to get your phones out now.'

'I don't believe you,' Rap growls while taking out her phone.

The wall pivots open slightly. 'Play your ringtones! There should be another hidden door on the other side of this. Let's go!'

Chapter 23

The next morning, Bran and I walk to the library to pick up the film equipment from Pascal, but I can barely keep my eyes open. We made it out of the tunnel—thank God, but we didn't see any of the missing people either.

Bran yawns loudly, covering her mouth with her hand. 'Jesus! I'm tired. Yesterday was a complete shit show, wasn't it, Wottie?'

'It was a disaster,' I reply. 'If only we had access to that report, then everyone would believe me...'

'Report or no report. I believe you, Wottie. If the Shriekers exists, why can't the white light exist too?'

'Thanks, Bran.'

We enter the library. Pascal's furry face lights up when he sees us. 'There you both are. I am glad that everyone got out of the tunnels safely. Are you very sure you want to continue with this investigation? Folkshore is becoming dangerous.'

'There's something going on,' I say. 'I think it's all linked, but I don't know how.'

'And Sherlock and Wottie never gave up,' Bran adds.

'If you're sure...' Pascal coughs as if his lungs are about to jump out. 'Oh, excuse me. This pesky cold doesn't seem to be budging.'

'Make sure you look after yourself, Pas.' Bran pats him on the back a bit too hard. 'Can't have you dying on me now.'

Pascal winces and carefully removes Bran's hand. 'No need to worry about me.' Pascal points to the equipment box on the front desk. 'Here's all the film equipment from the basement.'

I dig through the box, admiring the tripod, shotgun mic, lapel mics, lights and audio recorder. 'Thank you.'

Pascal rocks on his heels and grins. 'I'm glad it's going to good use rather than collecting dust.'

Bran is distracted by her phone.

'What did you want to tell me about the special book?' I whisper, moving away from Bran.

'Oh, I've found out a few intriguing details about the tablet from my contacts. Allegedly, it transforms things it's close to.'

'Transforms how? Does it change the appearance of things?' I ask, remembering the conversation I had with Eustace.

'Exactly that.'

'What else did you find out?'

'Not what but who.'

'Who?'

'Just spit it out,' Bran exclaims, hoisting herself onto the desk. 'You sound like bloody owls.'

'Guess who originally owned the tablet?' Pascal asks.

'Wh—'

'I swear to God,' Bran mutters under her breath.

'Duke. Everbee.'

I gasp then laugh, realising how dramatic I'm acting. 'Are Duke and Alice Everbee related, by any chance? She's Mal's friend from Whitemount.'

Tapping his wet nose, Pascal replies, 'Bingo. Alice is Duke's daughter. On the off chance that Alice's inbox is still active, I have sent her an email. There's definitely a mystery here.'

Chapter 24

Red and Cindy help me set up the lighting for Grandma Pat and Auntie Pauline's interviews. Red's cottage may be in Folkshore, but the inside reminds me of my home back in Kent, especially with all of Red's framed baby photos.

Red's phone pings and she checks it, typing a quick response using her nails.

'Is that Rap again?' I ask, adjusting the height of the tripod. 'What are they saying about Westley?'

'Yeah,' Red replies, not looking up. 'She's there, but the police won't let her see him yet.'

'And Roland is still not helping?' Auntie Pauline asks, puzzled. 'What is he there for if he can't help us?'

'I *tried* to speak to him about Westley, but he kept telling me to leave Folkshore.' Cindy rummages through her bag to retrieve her phone. 'Maya downloaded this app on my phone—it recorded the whole conversation. Let me play it.'

'Cinderella, please. Will you listen to me, for goodness' sake? I can get you and the girls out. You need to leave Folkshore! It's all getting out of control—I should never have gotten involved. Folkshore can't be saved. It's all a mess.'

'What is a mess?' Cindy asked. 'What's going on?'

'I wanted more for Folkshore, but it can't be stopped. You're a big fool if you don't listen. You and that vigilante group you're associating yourself with. As I said before, there's nothing to be done and there's nothing more I can do to help you.'

'Folkshore is our home! You might be able to give up on it, but I can't. Look at what Folkshore has become. What about all the missing people? We both know that Westley isn't the mastermind behind all of this. What are you hiding?'

'I've given you all the time I can. I'm late for my next appointment. Please greet my granddaughters for me, since you won't allow me to see them.'

Cindy pauses the audio. 'Something is definitely happening, and he knows about it, but he won't talk about it with me.' Cindy dumps her phone in frustration. 'He almost sounded sorry at the beginning of the conversation, but he soon went back to his normal self.'

Grandma Pat shakes her head in disgust. 'This is why you shouldn't give certain people too much power—they can't handle it. I hope Roland remembers where he's from, and fast.'

'And if he doesn't, I will go down there and whip him myself,' Auntie Pauline adds, laughing. 'Roland's not too grown for licks.'

Red snickers. 'You wouldn't, Auntie Pauline.'

'Yes, I would.' Auntie Pauline nods. 'He better not try me. Now, enough about Roland. I'm ready for my close-up.'

Grandma Pat and Auntie Pauline are really out here in their Sunday best with their coloured trouser suits and matching church hats.

Auntie Pauline struggles to fix her lopsided hat. 'What are you laughing at? Don't we look good?'

Red sniggers and Auntie Pauline kisses her teeth.

'Don't listen to Red,' I say, taking a picture of Grandma Pat. 'You *both* look good.' Lowering my camera, I sit down on the sofa in front of them. 'So, I'm going to ask you a few simple questions. Do whatever feels natural.'

Auntie Pauline blows through her nostrils in response. 'Don't you worry about us. When I was your age, I ran things, you know.' She points to herself.

I swear parents recycle the same lines because my parents say the exact same thing. Mum swears that she taught me how to dress, but then she wears silver turtlenecks with zebra-print trousers.

I zoom in, focusing the camera on the two women seated on the couch, and imagine what the audience will see. One matriarch with years of experience and one woman close to my mum's age, in her prime.

'How long have you lived in Folkshore?' I ask.

Grandma Pat speaks first, but she isn't looking at the camera, so I signal to her, pointing to my camera.

'I'll be celebrating my fiftieth year in Folkshore soon.' She flashes her teeth in a smile. 'I raised my children and grand-children here.'

'What was it like for you, coming to Folkshore from London?' I ask. 'And what was it like coming to London?'

'I came over from Jamaica to London in the sixties. It was very different to what I was used to,' Grandma says.

'And colder,' Auntie Pauline adds. 'I *never* got used to that cold.'

'That's right, Pauline.' Grandma Pat laughs breathlessly. 'I remember leaving Jamaica to stay with my auntie in London, and everyone would ask, "How is it? How's the weather? I've heard that it snows there." It was a very different time. Do you know what my mother always told me? That I should never forget where I was from. And I haven't.'

My mum tells me that too. I could *never* forget.

'We started our own community in London and lived life regardless of what some people said,' Auntie Pauline says, bopping to imaginary music. 'When I used to go dancing, they were jealous because they couldn't move like us. Stiff like cardboard.'

Grandma Pat chokes with laughter, and we have to take a short break for her to catch her breath.

Back on camera, they have a long conversation about life in London and Folkshore.

'Folkshore is a community,' Grandma Pat says. 'When I first came, it was a beautiful place to live. I was shocked at first by the animals and nature and things, but they all worked together with the Hometree at its centre. Folkshore wasn't perfect, but it worked. When the people are good, then the environment is blessed, and it's like God is smiling down at us.'

'Folkshore is special to you. What do you think about the Assembly and their plans for Folkshore?'

Auntie Pauline shakes her head. 'Oh, don't get me started on them...'

After around two hours of filming, I have more than enough footage.

'Look at the likes and comments your photo of the train station got,' Red says, showing me her phone. She scrolls down through the thousands of comments under the post.

> ### I thought it was under construction
> 👍 145 👎 ❤ REPLY

> ### trapping us in here like animals
> 👍 294 👎 ❤ REPLY

> ### the Assembly should be abolished
> 👍 502 👎 ❤ REPLY

> ### why do they keep lying to us?
> 👍 109 👎 ❤ REPLY

As I'm packing my equipment away, something Grandma Pat said reminds me of the redacted report about Folkshore. 'Grandma Pat, what did you mean before? You said that when people are good, then the environment is blessed.'

'When you've been here for as long as I have, you'll see that when things aren't right with the community, Folkshore isn't right,' she replies. 'Everything works in harmony.'

I'm reminded of Pascal's words. *'From what I can decipher, it is an investigation into Folkshore's ecosystem.'*

'So, you think there could be a direct link between the people and Folkshore?' I ask, wondering how true that report could be. *There's a story here.*

'What are you thinking, honey?' Cindy asks.

'The report that Red found... I know some of us think it's useless, but everything the Assembly said is a lie. What if that report can tell us more about what's happening?'

'But we need an ID card to get inside the restricted area and read the full report. My father isn't the most cooperative man when he's not getting his way.'

'Why don't we try to get the report ourselves?'

Cindy bites her lip before replying, 'There is another problem. Lavinia. She works at the town hall and she truly hates me.'

How can anyone hate Cindy?

'I have an idea.'

Chapter 25

Cindy and I huddle outside the town hall, waiting for Bran and Prince.

Cindy shivers. 'Thank God—they're here.'

'You missed me didn't you, Wottie?' Bran says. 'That's why you didn't call Riding Hood or Rap to help you.'

'No,' I reply. '*Red* was busy working on stuff for the documentary and Rap is still mad at me because I didn't tell anyone about the Shriekers and almost got us killed.'

'Why? That was *years* ago.'

'Days, Bran,' Prince comments as he ties his long blond hair into a bun. 'What do ya need from me?'

Bran winks, making rude gestures. 'Go on, Fols. Tell him what you need.'

'Next time I'm not calling you,' I reply, climbing up the stairs to the town hall. 'You just need to distract Lavinia, that's it.'

'I know what to do. I'm a natural!' Bran yells, stomping up the steps behind me.

'A natural pain in the arse for sure,' Prince says.

Lavinia is *just* as Cindy described, but she forgot to mention that Lavinia is a parrot.

'Cinderella, is that you? You're looking worn out,' Lavinia squawks, waddling forward to greet us. She's wearing a turquoise trouser suit and pink lipstick.

Immediately, my gaze zooms in on the ID card clipped to her right blazer pocket.

Cindy grinds her teeth before putting on a forced smile. 'How are you doing, Lavinia? We're here to see the records in the Albany Room.'

Cindy literally ruffles Lavinia's feathers.

'Cinderella,' she squawks. 'You should know that the Albany Room is restricted to *privileged* eyes only. If you hadn't left your father high and dry, he would give you access.'

Then Bran falls to the floor. She rolls around, gripping her leg, right by the 'wet floor' sign. 'My leg!'

'Branna!' Cindy reaches down to her, trying not to laugh. 'Honey, are you alright? I hope it's not broken.'

'I've cracked my pulonomy artery!' Bran whimpers.

I roll my eyes. Bran *definitely* got a D in GCSE Drama.

'Lavinia, are you going to do something about this?' Cindy asks, baiting her.

'Oh no!' Lavinia squeals, her feathers pulled close to her body. 'Oh no!'

As Lavinia bends down, Prince swipes the card from her blazer pocket and sidles out of sight. Bran rolls further into the centre of the foyer and Lavinia waddles after her. I follow Prince, ducking out of the range of any cameras, until we reach a bland pumpkin-coloured door with no signs.

I thought the door would be guarded since it's restricted. 'Are you sure this is the Albany Room?'

'Yup, it's what Pascal described.' Prince presses the ID card against the small black box at the side of the door, and it buzzes open.

The Albany Room is a plain room filled with rows of shelves.

Prince bends in front of a tablet perched on a holder in the centre of the room. 'It's a catalogue system. What's the name of the article again?'

'An investigation into the spectral phenomena of Folkshore.'

'Got it. It's under AL5:7773.'

'This is *much* easier than I thought it would—'

'Doncha dare say it, don't even think it,' Prince warns.

'Fine,' I say, searching for the reference number on the shelves. 'Are you sure that's the right number? There is nothing here after AL4.'

'AL5:7773,' Prince repeats. 'Hold on. It says it's in Albany Room 2.'

'Where's that?'

Prince points to another pumpkin-coloured door tucked in the far corner of the room. 'Must be over there.'

I take the card from Prince and press it against the box

by the door, but it buzzes and flashes red. I pull hard on the handle, but the door won't open.

'Told ya not to say it.'

'Pascal was right,' I groan, hitting the door. 'We're going to have to get Roland's card.'

I thought we were finally going to get some answers and figure out what's been going on, but nothing in Folkshore is ever simple.

'That report must be important if they're hiding it in there,' Prince says, stepping away from the door. 'We have to go. We've been ages.'

We slip out of the room, heading back towards Bran. She is resting on a chair in the corner while Cindy fans her.

'I'm healed! It's a miracle.' Bran hops up from the chair when she sees us.

'What about your leg?' Lavinia squeals, ruffling her feathers. 'You could be seriously injured. Wait!'

After we're safely outside, Cindy looks at us, wide-eyed and eager. 'Did you find it? I can't believe we got one over on Lavinia.'

'Er, Cindy,' I start.

Seeing my face, she groans. 'I thought we could do this without my father.'

'We know where the report is. It's in a room off the Albany Room. But the card wouldn't let us into the second room,' I reply. 'Do you know what? Let's just forget about it. I bet it's not that important.'

I'm lying.

'She's lying,' Bran announces. 'We need to work on that.'

'No, we're going to get that report.' Cindy pulls me into a side hug. 'If you think it's important, then I do too.'

'Pas. Pas!' Bran shouts into her phone. 'I can't hear you. Nah, Fola couldn't get in with the card... Pas, what's going on? Can you hear me? Pas! I'm gonna call an ambulance.'

'Something's wrong,' Prince says.

Further up the road, Folkshorians lie still on the ground, reminding me of my vision, but this time it's only the animals on the ground.

Chapter 26

In the library, Pascal is on a stretcher by the front desk, a paramedic securing an oxygen mask around his face.

Bran rushes forward. 'Pas, are you alright?'

Using his oxygen mask, Pascal takes a few ragged breaths and nods.

'Will he be okay?' Cindy asks. 'We saw some other Folkshorians lying on the ground outside too. What's wrong with them? Do you know what's going on?'

The paramedics lift the stretcher. 'We're going to get him help, but we don't know exactly what's happening,' one of them replies. 'Who is riding with us in the ambulance?'

When the people are good, then the environment is blessed, and it's like God is smiling down at us.

'She is,' I answer for Bran, who's speechless for the first time in her life.

Pascal grips Bran's hand and removes his mask. 'I... won't... die on you. Promise.'

She squeezes his paw back. 'You better bloody not.'

We watch them load Pascal into the back of the midnight-blue ambulance. Bran climbs in too.

'Let's take my car to the hospital,' Cindy says.

The waiting room is overflowing with Folkshorians; worry is etched on their faces. My mind drifts to Deji. Are my family waiting to hear how his surgery went? Are they worried like I am now?

'Snacks?' Prince asks, heaving himself off his chair.

I follow him, to give myself something to do. If Priya was here, she would make me get her a pack of M&M's. I miss her.

Prince chooses a pack of sweets from the vending machine. I'm more used to seeing a cigarette resting between his fingers.

'No smoking today?'

Tearing the packet open, Prince empties half the sweets into his mouth and chews. 'I'm trying to quit. Apparently, they're not good for you.'

'You don't say,' I tease.

'There you two are,' Cindy pants, hurrying over to us. 'We can go in to see Pascal now.'

Bran is waiting outside the door. I nudge her with my shoulder, trying to get her to smile. 'He'll be alright, Sherlock.'

'Too right he will, Wottie.' Bran cracks a smile.

Pascal is in bed, with a female badger sitting beside him. She has a cropped hairstyle dyed white to match her fur.

'Sherlock, this is Jackie—Pascal's wife.' Bran hugs the badger and Cindy whispers something to her. The beeping of the machine fills the room. Pascal is taking deep breaths. Jackie's fur bunches around her eyes as she smiles. 'Thanks so much for coming.'

Pascal coughs.

'Take it easy, my love.' Jackie reaches over to pick up a glass of water from the bedside table. 'Here—drink some of this.' She moves Pascal's mask to one side so he can sip the water.

The door creaks open and Dr Ida pops her head through the door. 'Hi, I'm Dr Ida. We're going to take Pascal for some more tests now, which should last a few hours. If you're family, you can wait in the family room and someone will come and get you once we're done.'

'Thanks so much, Doctor,' Jackie responds, shouldering a white tote bag. 'Branna, why don't you go with Cindy and I'll call you when I have any updates? I don't want you cooped up in here.'

Bran is about to argue, but Pascal says her name.

'I'll be... fine... go,' he croaks.

'Yes,' Cindy says, rubbing Bran's arm. 'Let's go back to my flat.'

'Alright,' Bran replies reluctantly.

'I just... w-want to talk to Fola... for... a... second before you go.'

Everyone leaves the room.

Pascal struggles to sit up. 'Listen... to me. I continued digging... about... *The Chr*—'

'*The Chronicles of Folkshore,*' I finish.

'I found out something... I wasn't supposed to know... The tablet has guardians because of... how... special it is. The guardians... protect... it... from... getting into the w-wrong hands, and... different families are... entrusted to look after it.'

'Did you figure out how it ended up in the auction?'

'No.' Pascal coughs. 'Duke was... its last owner... and... water. Please. I... need water.'

I grab the glass from the table. Some of the water spills over the side before Pascal's lips grip the straw. 'I... don't... know how it got to the auction... but technically Rumpelstiltskin is its new guardian.'

'Are you ready for your tests now, Pascal?' Nurse Rose asks, peeping her head through the door. 'Sorry for interrupting.'

'Wait...' Pascal clutches my arm, making me lean closer. 'Alice... emailed. She said... about... the Assembly... Whitemount... she wants to video... chat with you.' He pushes a piece of paper into my hand just before Nurse Rose wheels him away, taking the answers with him. Alice's number is scrawled on the paper. I don't waste any time messaging her.

Me

Hi Alice

I'm Pascal's friend. When do you want to video call?

'I've got some news,' Cindy says as I leave the hospital room. 'My father has agreed to meet me.'

Chapter 27

The next day, we're in Cindy's bakery. She's plating up finger sandwiches and cake for us. Cindy offered her dad afternoon tea with the girls as a bribe, so he would come around.

'Are you sure about this?' I ask for the tenth time. 'You don't have to do this.'

'Yes, I am *very* sure,' Cindy whispers so the girls won't hear. 'You need that report and I need answers. Now, let's do this interview before my nerves get the better of me. Don't forget that my father keeps his cards in the top pocket of his suit.'

Maya holds up a small mirror to her mum's face. Cindy pulls down at the non-existent bags under her eyes. 'It looks like I haven't slept—and am I dressed properly for this?'

I focus my camera and give Cindy a once-over. She has on a fitted green turtleneck and flared blue jeans.

'I chose Mum's outfit,' Maya says smugly, snapping the mirror shut. 'Now pleeease can I be in the film?'

'Having the girls in it would be cute, actually,' I mumble to myself, trying to figure it out.

I feel eyes on me.

My eyebrows raise in confusion. 'What?' I ask and start mumbling to myself again. 'I think you should let the girls be in it. It'll be cute. It only has to be for a second.'

'Okay, but only for a second,' Cindy agrees.

'Yes!' Maya cries, bouncing up and down. She shrugs off her coat to reveal a midnight-blue dress with a sequined gold firework design.

I want to be Maya when I grow up.

'Can you stand here with this?' I hand them a clapperboard each. 'All you need to do is open and close it. Maya, you walk that way and Dani, you that way. You got it?'

'Hmmm,' Maya says. 'Are you sure my role isn't bigger?'

'No,' I reply. 'Let's try it. And... go.'

Maya stands in front of her sister with her arms spread wide. 'Welcome to Cinderella Asamoah's interview. I'm Maya Asamoah, her favourite daughter.'

'Cut!' I yell, trying not to laugh. 'Maya. Just do your part like I said. Okay?'

'Fineeee.' She stamps her sparkly gold pumps on the floor.

The next take is also a failure, as they run into each other and Dani starts crying. We finally get it, and by then Cindy is super relaxed because she's been laughing.

'What does Folkshore mean to you?' I ask her.

Cindy pauses for a second. 'It means so much. Folkshore was where I fell in love. Folkshore also means opportunity. It's where my love of baking was born, and where Pumpkin Time was made. Folkshore was where my grandma taught me how to cook. I would bother her in the kitchen as she made all these amazing treats. She taught me how to make bofrot and chin chin too, so it had that crunch. She used to sneak me all these treats behind my father's back. I wish my daughters could've met her.'

She's silent for a while, several emotions washing over her face. 'When I moved back here, I got a small business grant. Thanks to that and the money from my late husband, this place was born.' She bites her bottom lip and looks down. 'It's been hard. But the local business owners around here have been a blessing to me. I'm now head of the local business committee and I'm so proud of everything we're doing, but it seems as though the Assembly won't rest until there is no more Folkshore left.'

Soon it's time to wrap up. As I'm packing my equipment away, Roland strides through the door, wearing a fresh suit and looking relaxed, as if Folkshore isn't in chaos.

Cindy mouths to the girls, 'Best behaviour.'

'Hello, Cinderella,' Roland says, regarding her coolly. 'And look at my beautiful granddaughters. Both of you have grown so much, and you're smart too, I bet.'

'Can't say the same about you,' Cindy mutters under her breath.

I laugh into my hand.

'Yes, they have, haven't they? Why don't you take a seat, Father?'

Then my phone goes off.

Bran

> It's freezing
>
> we're waiting for you

A message from Alice comes in as I'm about to put my phone away.

0893 393 3939

> Yes, that would be good.
> Are you free for a call
> tomorrow?

Me

Yes

Roland unbuttons his blue suit jacket and sits down. 'What an amazing spread. You were always so talented—just like my mother. It's too bad that you're so preoccupied with your *unsavoury* associations, but if you promise me that you're done with them, I will personally see to it that nothing happens to your bakery.'

'What do you mean by that?' Cindy asks, grinding her teeth. 'Is something going to happen to the bakery?'

'Easy,' I whisper. Cindy takes a step back from her dad.

'Nothing will happen if you act right.' Roland slathers jam onto a scone and takes a messy bite. 'I can fix it all for you and get you back on track.'

Is this the same man who was scared and begging Cindy to leave Folkshore the other day? Who does he think he is?

Roland pauses, his knife in one hand, and points it at me. 'And you are?'

'This is Leah,' Cindy replies. 'She's been helping me out at the bakery, part-time. You know, since the Assembly have been kicking people out of their homes, people have been hungrier.'

'Granddad, would you like to see the story I wrote at school?' Maya asks, diverting attention towards her and away from her mum. Smart girl. 'My teacher said it was the best in the class.'

While Maya has Roland eating out of her hands, Cindy pulls me into the kitchen. She groans and slams the top cupboard shut. 'I can't do this. Are you hearing him? He's all "but I can fix it all for you and stop associating with them".'

'Just ignore him. I'll get the card.' Picking up the tray with the teas, I say, 'Now, smile. We've got stuff to steal.' I move back to the table and set the tray down. 'Who wants tea?'

'I'll take a peppermint tea, please,' Roland responds. 'Did you know that peppermint tea helps relieve tension, headaches and migraines?'

'You're giving me a headache right now,' Cindy mumbles.

As I hand Roland his cup, I *accidentally* trip and spill the headache-reducing peppermint tea all over his suit jacket.

'Oh, God!' Roland pulls off his jacket and glares at me. 'Look what you've done!'

'Sorry! I'll just take it to the kitchen and clean it for you.'

'Use detergent, vinegar and water to get that stain out!' he shouts.

I rush into the kitchen and check the top pocket, but it's empty. Where's his ID card?

'Wait!' Cindy shouts.

'It's in the inside pocket,' Roland says from behind me, a cold edge to his voice.

'It's not what it looks like,' I say, my stomach spinning.

'Yes, Father. Leah was just... er... making sure your pockets were empty before putting your jacket in the washing machine.'

Roland flexes his fingers into fists. The kitchen island is the only thing separating us. As he takes a step around it, I take a step the other way. There's no way I'm going to let him catch me.

'Save your lies, Cinderella.' Roland sneers. 'I *knew* she looked familiar. She's one of them, isn't she? She's part of the 'We are Folkshore' movement.'

Is that what they're calling us now?

'Yeah, I am,' I fire back. 'People are missing and dying, but the Assembly doesn't care. What are you doing to help? Has your special task force even been down into the tunnels yet to look for the missing people?'

'I told you to stop associating with them, Cinderella,' Roland scolds her. 'She's a thief.'

I lock eyes with Cindy, hoping she understands.

I throw his suit jacket across the room. Roland charges

around the island to grab it, but I'm halfway to the door, his ID card in my hand. I run through the door and Cindy slams the door behind me, locking Roland inside.

'Let me out, now! Cinderella!' Roland shouts. 'Is this any way to treat your father?'

Chapter 28

I run all the way to the town hall and let out a relieved breath when its Grecian columns come into view. Bran and Prince speak at the same time.

'What time you call this, Wottie?'

'Who you runnin' from?'

Out of breath and definitely dying, I try to get some words out. 'We... locked Roland in the back of the bakery.' I hold up the ID card. 'I got it.'

'Nice one,' Prince exclaims. 'Bran, ya know what to do.'

Bran marches into the town hall like she owns the place. As soon as Lavinia sees Bran, she squawks and her green feathers draw close to her body. 'No. Not you again!'

Prince and I creep around the edge of the foyer and disappear down the marble corridor.

'This report better be worth it, because Roland is coming after us,' Prince says once we've stopped outside the pumpkin-coloured door.

The black box buzzes when I touch the card on it. It works.

'Okay, here we go,' I say, touching the ID card to the box by the second door.

It flashes red.

'Flip it.'

It can't be that easy, but I try it. The door buzzes and flashes green.

'It really *is* that easy.' Prince chuckles, leaning over me to push the door open. 'After you, Princess.'

'Don't call me that, Charming.' Priya would probably be hyperventilating right now and planning a wedding.

Albany Room 2 has several powder-blue drawers against three walls.

'We're looking for AL5:7773,' I say, checking the first drawer to the right. Hurriedly we scan them, looking for the file that will, hopefully, answer some of our questions.

'Gotcha. AL5:7773,' Prince calls from the left-hand side of the room. 'An Investigation into the Spectral Phenomena of Folkshore.'

❧ ❧

We're back at Cindy's flat, sitting around her dining table, with the brown folder in the middle.

'And he still hasn't come back?' Bran asks Cindy.

'No.' Cindy laughs. 'My father is probably scared that people will find out that we outsmarted him.'

'He can bloody do one,' Bran adds. 'All of them can. We got what we wanted from him anyways.'

Rap crosses her arms, glaring at me. 'This had better be worth it. There are other things we could be doing.'

Prince moves the folder towards me. 'Do the honours, Fola.'

I open up the report and start reading for everyone to hear.

CONFIDENTIAL REPORT

AN INVESTIGATION INTO THE SPECTRAL PHENOMENA OF FOLKSHORE

FINDINGS

Samples provided of Folkshorians (test subjects A-F) indicate traces of the liquid substance 'Lx20', referred to here as 'white light', found in the original Folkshorian settlers and soil samples taken from the Hometree. Lx20 is known for its glowing properties. It is disseminated through pollen from trees and is ingested by Folkshorians. People or creatures who

are not native to Folkshore may react to
the pollen with symptoms that include
sneezing, itchy eyes and a runny nose.

It can be concluded that any harm to
Folkshorians can cause the destabilisation
of Folkshorian creatures and nature in
Folkshore, including its climate.
In times of destabilisation, the trees
release toxins, which results in cases
of paranoia, bursts of uncontrollable
anger, and sickness in Folkshorians.
Prolonged exposure to the toxins can
cause Folkshorians to go into a frenzy.
Continued destabilisation could be fatal
for Folkshore and all its inhabitants.

There is more to the report, but I stop reading to process.

'It all makes sense,' Red says, clicking her fingers together.

'What makes sense? Oh, so you actually believe this report?' Rap asks with a condescending smile. 'You wasted our time, Fola. This report is over 20 years old! It's useless.'

'It wasn't a waste of time,' I fire back. 'I told you all about the Shrieker collecting liquid from that man, and I'm sure it's the same glowing liquid that was dripping from the water tank in the room. It has to be Lx20.'

'I think Fola's right,' Red agrees. 'Ty moves mad sometimes, but it was never *this* bad. Rap, even you have been acting more...' She purses her lips.

'More what?' Rap snaps.

'Rude! You're *too* rude!'

'I'm always angry at the Assembly—we're not going to blame the trees or Folkshore for that. Who wouldn't be angry?' Rap asks. 'Look at what they're doing to Folkshore.'

'I'm siding with Wottie,' Bran says, taking the report from my hand. 'Pas is sick and he's *never* sick—his fucking permanent cold only started this year. The report said Folkshorian creatures.'

'Ya can't deny that *something* is going on,' Prince adds.

'You all can't be this gullible!' Rap exclaims. 'This is obviously a game the Assembly are playing. They *knew* we would find the report. They're all murderers and liars who don't care about us!'

Cindy lays her palms flat on the table and speaks slowly. 'My father is *many* things, but he's *not* a murderer. He can't be. I know sometimes he doesn't show it, but deep down he knows what he's doing is wrong.'

The tension in the air is cut with pings and buzzes from our phones.

TEXT ALERT

THE 'WE ARE FOLKSHORE'
MOVEMENT IS PROHIBITED FROM
PROTESTING AS THE MEMBERS OF
THIS MOVEMENT ARE IN DIRECT
VIOLATION OF CURFEW. ANYONE
ASSOCIATED WITH THIS MOVEMENT
WILL BE PENALISED.

'Are you sure your dad knows that?' Rap asks, getting up from the table.

Cindy stares down at her phone. 'They're terminating the lease for my bakery because of my "unsavoury associations".'

Chapter 29

We leave Cindy's flat and go outside. There's a commotion outside Giselle's salon. Since the earthquake, the Assembly has been refurbishing the shops affected. Giselle's was one of them. What used to be Giselle's Hair and Beauty Palace is now a restaurant: the Blue Hen. You can tell it's an expensive restaurant from its cream décor and soft lighting, which reflects a golden glow off the wine glasses on the tables.

'Giselle, what's all this?' Red asks. 'I thought the insurance company was fixing up the salon. Did you sell your place to the Assembly too?'

'That's a foolish question.' Giselle kisses her teeth. 'Why would I sell the salon to them? The insurance company has been dodging my calls and I came in today to check on the shop. Evil works fast.'

'This isn't right. They can't do this.' Cindy leaves with her phone pressed to her ear, probably to call her dad.

Edward Hamilton creeps out from behind the restaurant, apparently attempting to leave unseen, but the shop owners corner him. Of course the Assembly is involved. Scowling,

Edward says, 'If you were found to be involved in that abhorrent "We are Folkshore" movement, you're in breach of your contract, and the Assembly are within their rights to terminate it.'

As usual, the police pigs emerge from wherever they have been hiding, ready to silence us.

'Which movement?' Giselle points at Edward. 'I'm not part of the movement! You better fix whatever you did to my salon, now!'

Smirking, Edward turns to Red. 'It would seem that your cousin *is* involved, and she's been seen leaving your salon on several occasions. How do we know that you're not conducting secret meetings inside?'

'That doesn't make sense,' Red argues. 'Giselle isn't part of it.'

'You can't have my salon!' Giselle yells, running towards the restaurant, but the officers trot forward, blocking her from getting near. They twist her arm behind her back to restrain her.

'You're hurting me!'

The other shop owners shout at the officers and Giselle continues to struggle, even though she's being restrained.

'Officer, you can let her go.' Edward smooths out his suit, checking for invisible wrinkles. 'There's nothing else to be done here.'

The officer lets Giselle go but warns her, 'If you're seen near these premises again, we'll lock you up for trespassing.'

Giselle staggers back as if someone has pushed her. 'Destiny, this is *your* fault. I told you not to get involved! Now look what's happened!'

'But Giselle—' Red starts.

'I don't want to hear it.' With one last look at the restaurant, Giselle marches off down the high street, taking Red's fight with her.

'They won't get away with this, Red,' Rap says calmly—too calmly. 'Message everyone to meet us here now.' Rap looks at the rest of us, seething. 'We'll show them.'

Within the hour, the high street is packed with people protesting against the Assembly.

'They can't silence us!' Rap roars.

'They can't silence us!' the crowd repeats. The atmosphere is electric.

'Watch what I'm gonna do.' With his hood up and a bat in his hand, Ty sprints down the street towards the junction. The crowd follow him, a blur of signs, bats, and hatred.

A jagged flash of lightning illuminates the sky, sending out threads of blue lightning that connect with the luminous trees. It reminds me of my vision.

'Who are we?' Rap cries, her clenched fist raised high.

'We are Folkshore!'

I'm lost in the crowd, separated from my friends, as we turn off onto Goblin Grove. I know where Ty is going. The dark sky crackles and rain pours from the heavens. Wetness drips off my body.

'Watch this!' Ty repeats, storming inside the lobby of the new fancy apartments. Others join him, destroying everything in sight.

The pigs appear in full face shields with batons between their hooves. Officer Levi trots forward, leading them.

'Get them back!' Office Levi bellows as they push against the crowd.

But the police aren't alone. A group of around 20 Shriekers emerges behind the police. The crowd murmurs, disbelief spreading as they attempt to make sense of what they're seeing. The Shriekers glide towards people in the crowd, picking them off one by one. They plunge the metal devices into the people's chests, draining Folkshorians of the white light.

'Use your phones!' I yell, avoiding a Shrieker at the last minute. 'Use your ringtones!'

My voice is drowned out by screams. I scramble for my phone, but it's dead.

'What the fuck do you think you're doing?' Ty threatens the police, charging towards them from the apartment with a bloody bat. 'You think you can just do what you want.'

Officer Levi's taser connects with a spark of lightning, creating a veiny electric charge in the sky. The taser darts hit Ty and he drops face-first to the ground. The officers cuff him while he's shaking.

'Ty!' Red screams.

The police drag his unconscious body up. Blood drips down his face, soaking his tracksuit. Officer Levi gnashes his crooked teeth at Red, the taser a live bomb in his hand. 'You don't want to end up like your boyfriend here.'

The rain seems to wash away Rap's fight. She steps back, and the protestors who are left retreat too. Rap, Red and I scatter into the night. When we reach the junction, we run down the high street to Cindy's door. I knock frantically, looking over my shoulder to make sure no police officers followed us here. 'Open the door, please! It's me.'

The door flies open, and Cindy lets out a huge breath. 'Oh, thank God. You're all okay. Come in quickly.'

'They have Ty,' Red cries, hiccupping.

Cindy tries to hug Red, but Red moves away. Wiping away her tears, Red hisses at Cindy with a spiteful expression on her face. 'It's the Assembly's fault. Your dad's fault. Do you even care?'

'What do you mean?' Cindy asks, her voice quivering. 'Red, honey. Of course I care. I care about all of you like you're my own daughters.'

'Don't chat to me, man!' Red pushes past Cindy and leaves the flat.

Like the wind, Rap rushes out after Red, leaving shivers in her absence. Cindy drops onto the sofa, her head in her hands.

Chapter 30

The streets are silent the next morning and the air is chilly. Discarded pieces of wood and signs litter the street. When I make my way to Red's, there is no one in sight, not even the police pigs.

Bran's name flashes on my screen and I answer her call, preparing for more problems.

'The bloody pigs are trotting around Greenwood like they own the place. Oi!' She breaks off to shout at the police. 'That's where I keep my thongs! Are you a paedo or something?'

'Why are they there?' I ask, groaning.

'They're investigating Greenwood. I heard them talking about "multiple persons of interest" living here.' Bran lowers her voice to a whisper. 'And they really wanted to see your room. It's good you're staying with Cindy. Where are you now?'

I thought they'd stopped looking for me, but I guess not.

'I'm going over to Red's, so we can figure out how to get Ty back.'

'Tell me what you're gonna do and I'll meet you after. Oi! Get your grubby hands off my Gucci. Bye, Wottie.'

This is all getting out of control. How is it that the bad people always have the most power?

I knock on Red's door, praying that we can figure out a way to get Ty back. It feels like we're never going to beat the Assembly.

'Who is it?' Grandma Pat asks from behind the door.

'Grandma Pat? It's me, Leah.' I hear the click of the door unlocking and the rattle of a door chain before she pulls it open and lets me in.

'You added a chain.'

'I heard what happened to Tyrone.' Grandma Pat tuts, shaking her head. 'The police can't come barging in here.'

Red watches me as I enter the living room. Her puffy face and red eyes tell me she hasn't slept. Rap perches on the end of the sofa, looking deep in thought.

Grandma Pat fusses over Red. 'You need to eat something, Destiny.'

Red sniffs, clutching her tissue. 'I can't, Grandma. They've got Ty and I don't know if I'm going see him ag—'

'Don't even say it,' Grandma Pat scolds Red softly. 'Don't even *think* it because that boy is coming back.'

Red nods miserably.

I wait for Grandma Pat to leave the room before asking my question, 'What's the plan to get Ty back?'

'All of this was for nothing,' Rap mumbles to herself. 'They're either trying to get rid of us or restrict us, but they never let us be us.' She rocks backwards and forwards.

'No,' I say. 'I didn't get trapped in Folkshore for nothing. We're going to go down there now and demand to speak to Ty. We can figure out the rest later.'

Red wipes her face with the back of her hand. 'Yeah, you're right. Why am I sitting here crying? Let's go and get my man back.'

I expected the police station to be busier with people trying to see friends or family, but it's empty. Red marches straight through the automatic doors towards the pig behind the desk, whose snout is buried in a newspaper.

Red taps her nails on the desk. 'My boyfriend Tyrone Campbell was arrested last night, and I want to know when he'll be released.'

The pig lowers the newspaper and snorts. 'Tyrone Campbell isn't here. He was released this morning. See for yourself.' The officer knocks the screen in front of him and turns it to face us.

'What?' Red says. 'If Ty was released, he would've called me.'

'I don't know what else I can tell you.'

Beside Ty's name are the two officers who signed for his release. Officer Levi and Officer Kelly. Rap cusses when she sees the names on the screen. Why did it have to be them?

Red's hands tremble as she stabs at her phone to call Ty. 'Please answer,' she whispers. 'Please answer.' She tries several times. Each time her call goes unanswered, her face crumbles more. Tears fill her eyes. 'Maybe he went to a friend's house,' she suggests weakly.

Rap slams the top of the desk, drawing the attention of other officers. 'Do you actually believe what you're saying? He's gone.'

Red storms out of the police station and paces up and down outside, her fists clenched. Something silver flashes at the bottom of the steps, catching my eye. I run down the steps and pick it up. It's a thin chain with a small silver wolf charm.

'That's Ty's.' Red comes over to me and takes the chain. She stumbles over her words. 'He would *never* take this off. His dad gave it to him before he moved here to live with Mal. They took him.' Red's voice is thick with emotion. 'They *really* took him.'

I look at Rap, but she's silent, so I try. 'We'll find him.'

'How?!' Red shouts.

'Rap, why aren't you saying anything?' I ask. 'Aren't you the one who always says they can't stop us?'

The vein on Rap's head throbs, dangerously close to bursting.

'It's Ty's dumb fault anyways!' Rap explodes. 'He doesn't think. Why did he start destroying those apartments? The police still haven't released Westley, but you're only worrying about your boyfriend.'

Red's head rotates around like she's one of those possessed dolls in the film. 'Don't chat to me no more! Now Westley is gone, you won't have no one because you don't know how to treat people. Giselle was right. I should *never* have gotten involved.' Red runs off down the street back towards her house.

'Rap—'

'This is none of your business,' she snaps, and storms off in the opposite direction.

Chapter 31

'Are you sure this is Rap's house?' I ask, staring at the pink door. 'It doesn't seem like she'd live somewhere so...'

'I know,' Prince replies, tugging his beanie further down on his head. 'But this is it. Are we going in? We can't stand here all day, Fola.'

'I was gone for, what? Like two hours, and everything's gone to shit?' Bran remarks.

I give two sharp knocks on the door. Rap's twin opens the door. He's not her actual twin, but they have the same head shape, height and lean build. The difference is that he's a man and has a warm smile on his face, which I've never seen on Rap's face. The way Rap moves, you would think she gave birth to herself.

'Hi,' Mr Rapunzel says, and his deep brown eyes widen when he sees Prince. 'Prince. How are you, my boy?'

'I'm all good, sir.' Prince's face transforms into his casual grin. 'How's it goin'?'

'All this business with the Assembly and the curfews. I don't know what's happening with Folkshore, but don't let me keep you out here,' he replies. 'Come on in. Rapunzel came back in a bad mood, but she won't tell me what's wrong.'

'Isn't she always in a bad mood?' Bran comments. I nudge her, but Mr Rapunzel chuckles.

We follow Rap's dad. Inside, the walls are dark pink and white with those modern ceiling lights you see in the magazines. Rapunzel's mum is working at the glass dining table at the corner of the living room.

'What are you guys doing here?' Rap asks from the doorway, her face twisted into a frown.

'It's about the tunnels,' I reply, watching her parents out of the corner of my eye.

Rapunzel gets the hint and steers us into the corridor. As soon as the living-room door closes behind us, I say, 'Red has gone down into the tunnels to look for Ty. She sent me this message.'

Red

> I'm not waiting for anyone
>
> I'm going back to that room in the tunnels to look for Ty.

Red is Rap's best friend, even though they're fighting right now. I would want to know if something happened to Priya so I could do something about it.

'She doesn't listen!' Rap rubs her head in frustration. 'Why would she go by herself?'

'You basically said her boyfriend was stupid,' Bran comments. 'Fola told me everything. If my best friend said that to me, I'd be bloody hurt too.'

'What about all the things she said to me?' Rap says, narrowing her eyes. 'No, she thinks she can figure it out by herself so let her do it then.'

'Are you goin' to let something as minor as a fight stop you from helping Red?' Prince asks. 'If ya say you don't care, then that's complete gobshite. You're forgetting what else could be down there with Red.'

'Fine.' Rap huffs and grabs her black combat jacket off the hook. 'You better remember the way, Fola.'

'You're not going anywhere until you tell me where Ty is!' Red shouts from the hidden room in the tunnels.

She is holding her phone up to film a haggard-looking Dr Eric. He has dark bags under his eyes and greasy hair. What's he doing here?

Red says to us, 'Dr Eric knows where Ty is, but he's refusing to tell me.'

His gaze flickers over to us. 'I don't know where Ty is. Can you talk to your friend, please? I can't help her.' Dr Eric darts forward to grab Red's phone, but she moves out of the way just in time.

A piercing shriek sounds from outside the room and a vision comes to me, but it's hazy. I'm standing in the tunnel. Lots of shadowy bodies are in front of me, as a man walks by in a navy suit. The Shriekers surround him. The sound is distorted so I can only make out a couple words. *'Freedom... I can get you... no... tunnels. Deal.'*

Like the other visions, it's gone in a second, leaving me thinking about who the man is and what kind of deal he made with the Shriekers.

Rap glares at Dr Eric. 'Start speaking. Now.'

Staggering back, Dr Eric trips over his feet. 'Wait, wait,' he begs. 'It's not what it looks like. It is... but I had to. I made a deal with him. I *had* to do what he said. I can't tell you anything else—I'm sorry.'

'Is it Roland?' I ask. The man in my vision wore a similar suit to the one Roland wore before. 'Is he the boss?'

'I'm sorry, I can't say anything else.'

Hot tears fall down Red's face as she shouts, 'I swear to God! Tell us where they took Ty or I'm going to upload this.'

'Please don't upload it,' Dr Eric pleads. 'If you stop recording, I'll tell you. Please. He can't know I've told you this.' Dr Eric's pink tongue pokes out, licking his chapped lips. 'Please. Just lower the camera.'

Red lowers the phone and stops the video.

Dr Eric's shoulders sag as he breathes out. 'Tyrone *was* here, but he has been moved because this place has been compromised. I have no idea where he is now. I came down here to make sure that everything was gone. My job is just to monitor people down here—that's all. I swear to you all, I don't know where the second room is. Please.'

Rap frowns. 'What second room?'

Chapter 32

I unroll the blueprints on the table in the community centre. 'Before you guys say anything, I can't tell you who gave them to me because I don't want to get them in trouble.' I circle the point on the blueprints where the first room is and circle several other points. 'This is where the first room is, but it's empty. Here are some other spots where the second room could be.'

'We're going back down there,' Red says, smoothing down her faded red hair.

'I'll spread the word and gather some volunteers,' Mal replies. 'We need to find my nephew. The Assembly's special task force isn't doing anything.'

Rap inspects the blueprints. 'We have to be prepared this time. We need more flashlights and more phones in case we run into those Shriekers again.'

While they discuss what to do next, Alice Everbee's pale, heart-shaped face pops up on my phone screen.

'Sorry I couldn't meet before, Alice,' I apologise. 'There's been a lot going on.'

'*No worries at all, Fola. I was glad to get Pascal's email,*' she replies. '*I'm sorry to hear that he's in the hospital. I wanted to talk to you about the Assembly. You shouldn't trust them and their investors. When I moved to Whitemount a year ago, it had already started changing because of their investment. Hightower completely changed Whitemount, and most of the owners were bought out or pushed out. I've sent you some pictures so you can see what Whitemount looks like now.*'

Photos pop up one by one. They look similar to what Folkshore is becoming, with flashy apartments and restaurants replacing community shops.

'I knew it,' Rap says, clenching her fists.

'*My dad tried to stop the investment from going through in Folkshore, but he was murdered. The police say that Jack did it, but I don't think he did. It changed my dad. All of it did.*'

'What do you mean?' I ask.

'*My father was a good man.*' Alice's voice is strong, unwavering. '*He started to change the subject any time I brought up the Assembly's plans. He was different. He was scared.*' Alice's hazel eyes focus on mine through the screen. '*My dad said he had something to show me at the house. It was about the Assembly and the regeneration scheme. But I was busy and didn't go over to see him until it was too late. I know the Assembly did something to him. If there's anything to find, you need to go to our house. It will be there.*'

Chapter 33

The crash of thunder roars in my ears and lightning illuminates the dark sky.

'This is the place. Number 25 Bramble Place,' Prince says. 'Alice said the key is under the plant pot.'

Duke's front garden resembles a jungle. Weeds have taken over.

Bran flips a pot with the toe of her boot. 'There are, like, 50 bloody plant pots here. I know why the others didn't want to come now.'

We dig through the wet grass, lifting up random pots, unearthing clusters of yellow spiders until Prince eventually finds the key.

The rusted key opens the front door. We enter to see what looks like a crime scene. Books are scattered everywhere, the coffee table is in pieces, the TV is smashed, and the sofa is ripped to shreds. Prince whistles in surprise.

'What exactly are we looking for?' Bran asks, kicking rubbish away.

'Alice thinks her dad left something for her in this house. It was about the Assembly and the regeneration scheme.'

We split up. I search the back rooms while Bran and Prince search the front. I rummage through the drawers, then check the wardrobes, underneath the beds, and every other space in between.

'You found anything?' I shout.

'Nothing,' Prince calls back.

I try the study. In the centre of the desk is an incomplete model of Folkshore, like the one at the town hall exhibition, but something about it isn't right.

'Watcha got there?' Prince asks from behind me.

I point at a spot on the model. 'Shouldn't the Undercroft be there?'

Prince bends closer to the model and swears. 'They're replacing the Undercroft with a feckin' car park.' He takes out his phone and takes some photos.

Alice's number flashes up on my screen, and I answer, 'Hi, Alice. We've found this incomplete model of Folkshore, but nothing else.'

She sighs deeply over the phone. *'Thanks for letting me know. I haven't been there since after the funeral. Can you do me a favour, please? In my father's study, on the left-hand shelf above the chair, there are some videos he shot. They're saved on DVDs. There's one in particular I'm looking for. It's called "Alice's graduation". Can you see it?'*

I scan the titles on the DVDs, but I can't see it. 'I'm sorry, Alice. I don't think it's here.'

'*Are you sure? It should be there. What videos can you see?*'

'Beehive, Santorini, Mum's 70th, Alice at Thorpe Park, Tobi's recital—'

'*Wait, wait. What was that one?*'

'You mean Tobi's recital?'

'*No, the one before that. The Thorpe Park one. He never took me to Thorpe Park. I don't like rides because I'm afraid of heights. Can you check what's on that one?*'

I pull the DVD case off the shelf. 'Is there a DVD player in here?'

'You mean this one?' Bran answers, holding up a busted DVD player. 'Cindy's 40. She should have a DVD player. Let's go and find out.'

'Jesus, Bran.' Prince laughs. 'Cindy is only 33, and there's a DVD player at the community centre.'

'*Oh God. I hope this is something,*' Alice says.

I hope so too.

We're back at the community centre. Prince swipes the DVD off the table and puts it in the player. I call Alice back and put her on loudspeaker so she can hear whatever we find.

'Alice, we're playing the video now.'

Duke Everbee's face pops on the screen, looking dull-eyed and nervous. He fiddles with the camera multiple times before speaking. '*If you're watching this, Alice, then something has happened to me.*'

'*Oh my God, it's him.*' Alice weeps. '*It's really my father.*'

'*The Assembly know I'm about to come clean about their fake regeneration plans. Someone needs to stop them. I've been trying, but I'm outnumbered. Listen to me, Alice. They're turning Folkshore into a sanctuary for the rich. New Haven. They want to get rid of Folkshore as we know it.*'

Prince pauses the video and we sit in silence for a second before everyone starts talking at once.

'*I knew it. I knew it,*' Alice repeats.

Rap says, 'They can't cover this one up.'

'Yeah,' Red agrees. 'This is the evidence we need.'

'I can't believe my father's involved with this,' Cindy rages, slipping out of the room.

'Wait,' Prince interrupts. 'There's more.'

'*Alice, there's something else I need to tell you. I'm so sorry I couldn't tell you more about this myself, but I ran out of time. You're now the rightful guardian of* The Chronicles of Folkshore.'

'Isn't that the tablet you and Pas are always whispering about?' Bran asks, realisation settling in. 'It's why you wanted us to go to Rumpel's house.'

The others look confused. I nod, trying to process what I'm hearing.

'*I know I never told you about it properly, but there are chosen guardians of the book, and I... you are one of them. If you don't have the book, it may have slipped into the wrong hands. It's sacred. It chronicles the history of Folkshore. Anything that concerns Folkshore will be noted down in the* Chronicles. *It sees all.*'

Chapter 34

The Chronicles of Folkshore. At approximately 7:45 Folkshore Standard Time, an unidentified person enters Folkshore with a black bag on their back. This unidentified person is called Fo...

'Fola,' I whisper to myself. 'It's me.'

'Wottie, we know who you are,' Bran says, patting my arm. 'You told us, remember?'

'It's the words in my head!' I exclaim, hitting the table. Everyone shrinks back. 'Sorry, I heard these words in my head when I arrived in Folkshore. I think they're from the book. It was saying what was happening. The words appeared in my head out of nowhere.'

'What words?' Bran asks.

'*The Chronicles of Folkshore. At approximately 7.45 Folkshore Standard Time, an unidentified person enters Folkshore with a black bag on their back. This unidentified person is called Fo—* It must have been about me! If the book is really real, then I heard the words.'

'*If* it's real,' Rap starts, rubbing her head, 'then that could be how the officers knew to look for someone with the name starting with Fo. They must have the book.'

'Or they know someone who does.'

Alice clears her throat, drawing our attention back to her. 'And you didn't hear anything else? The words just stopped?'

'Yeah. I haven't heard anything since that.'

'Where could the book be?' Alice thinks out loud. 'And Rumpelstiltskin said the book had been stolen?'

'Yeah, that's what he *said*...' I reply.

'Rumpel is a collector.' Prince drags a hand through his hair. 'He could've been lying. If the book is watcha think it is, he might not want to let it go.'

Bran says, 'Don't you remember? He was acting dodgy when you asked him about it.'

'They're organising a ball,' Cindy states, marching back into the room. 'The Assembly are organising a ball. I just rang my father again and got his assistant. He told me everything.'

Red crosses her arms to hold her shoulders, and leans her chin on the table. 'I'm so tired. The Assembly can't find the missing people, but they can hold a ball.'

Cindy collapses into a chair. 'And it's not just *any* ball. It's a masked ball for the investors.'

'Hightower,' Alice says.

'How do we get in?' I ask. 'This could be our chance to speak to the investors about what they're doing to Folkshore.'

'One step ahead of you,' Cindy replies. 'His assistant is *very* chatty, and he thought that, since I was Roland's daughter, I

241

was invited anyways. I may or may not have told his assistant that I misplaced my tickets.'

'Nice one.' Prince grins.

'I need a lighter, a hairband and a bottle of Baileys Irish Cream.' She winks at Prince. 'I'll get the answers out of them.'

Prince holds up his hands. 'I want no part in this.'

'I couldn't get enough tickets for all of us, so the rest of you will have to be in the serving crew. Sorry,' Cindy says.

'What about extra photographers?' I ask. 'I can bring my camera.'

'Good idea, honey. I'll call my father's assistant and ask about it.'

Red taps her phone. 'Everyone's waiting at the Undercroft. Are we still going?'

'Oh yeah, I completely forgot about that,' I reply, thinking through everything that has happened. 'After today, we'll have enough footage for the documentary.'

'Enough to stop the Assembly,' Rap adds.

'Keep me posted,' Alice says before ending the call.

Carrying the box of film equipment, we leave the community centre for the Undercroft.

'You know what I'm going to do when all this is done, and we find Ty?' Red says. 'I'm going to get my grades and go to Jamaica to see my parents. All of this stress, yeah. It's not for me. What are you going to do after all this?'

'I'm going home,' I state simply. And I'm going to tell my parents that I want to study film and photography at sixth form. After almost dying here, I'll risk my mum threatening to send me to Nigeria, or that I'll end up working in Odeon.

The Undercroft is alive with skaters, bikers, artists and others who don't want to see another part of Folkshore stripped away.

'Catch!' Prince shouts, chucking a folded-up T-shirt at me. 'Check the back.'

Holding the black T-shirt up against my body, I admire the #WeAreFolkshore design on the front before flipping it around. The word 'director' is on the back. 'Thanks, Prince.'

The others remove their coats to reveal their own #WeAreFolkshore T-shirts. When did Prince have time to make these?

'There's always time to recognise talent,' Prince says, tapping his own personalised hoodie.

Using my camera, I track the skateboarders and bikers, watching their moves and anticipating their next ones for some action shots. I change the shutter speed, freezing the action and capturing some of their quicker moves.

Prince skates in front of me before heading towards the ramp. He propels himself off, doing a 360 flip in the air before landing. 'Woo!' he yells, throwing his hands in the air.

'Can all the skaters, bikers and artists sit on the ramp?' I ask.

As the ramp fills up, I look through the camera to check how the group is framed before addressing them. 'I'm going to ask you a few questions about Folkshore.'

'Make sure you get my good side,' Chris jokes, flipping his hair.

'And which side is that?' I ask, tilting my head.

A series of 'ooooohs' fills the space and soon they're all joking with each other.

'Okay, first question. When did you all come to Folkshore?'

'I was born here.'

'Same.'

'I'm just bunking with a friend—'

'Yeah, and you need to stop bunking with me and get your own place!'

'Why is the Undercroft so important to you?' I ask.

'Even if you don't know anyone, you can come here and vibe,' Chris answers.

Mia teases, 'Yeah, and you can just exist, until Chris bothers you.'

'You all love me!' Chris jokes.

I say something that I know will get a reaction. 'What if I told you that the Assembly are planning to get rid of the Undercroft?'

'What!?'

'I knew it! It was only a matter of time.'

'We can't let them get away with this. This is Folkshore.'

'I kinda thought this place would be around forever, though. It's part of Folkshore's history.'

I ask the group a few more questions. The time flies by. 'We're almost done. I want you all to shout, "We are Folkshore". Okay, one, two, three.'

'We are Folkshore!' they shout together.

'Thanks, everyone. Are you ready, Mia?'

'Yup,' she replies, pulling down the sleeve of her white jumper.

Not only is Mia a talented artist, but she also does spoken word. She's written a piece about the regeneration plans.

We're shooting deep in the Undercroft's tunnels, the graffiti artists spray-painting in the background. Mia's black-lined lips move, reciting the lines from her poem. 'How many takes have I got?'

'As many as you want.'

She smiles. 'Ready.'

In the final edit, the graffiti artists will be blurred in the background and Mia in focus as she performs.

> *Rivers. Of. Blood.*
> *Calloused hands*
> *grip the golden ticket,*
> *Union Jack intertwines*
> *with their ancestry*
> *in a hybrid contortion,*
> *Ghana Must Go*
> *bags leave marks of*
> *tension.*
>
> *Rivers.*

Rivers
of sweat,
of hardship,
scar bodies,
saddle their souls.

Like the wise man
who built his house on a rock,
they hammer in traditions.
Screw in wisdom.
Reinforce culture.

'Go back!'
they say.
Back to where?
When our blood
runs...

Chapter 35

'The account keeps freezing,' Red exclaims, showing me the thousands of likes on the documentary. 'Do you know how many messages have come in?'

'Good,' Rap says. 'We need as many people as possible out on the streets for the protest the day after tomorrow.'

We released the documentary this morning, and *everyone* is talking about it.

'Maybe it will scare the Assembly straight.' Cindy rolls a dusty brown suitcase into the living room and lays it down in front us. 'Just be careful at this ball. They might want to retaliate.'

'Let them try,' Rap taunts.

Cindy unzips the suitcase, which is full of dresses wrapped in protective plastic. 'Michael and I actually met at a ball, like the one you're going to tonight.' Cindy kneels down beside it; her fingers pause on the zip for a second as if she's trying to prep herself. 'My father was trying to schmooze the Assembly members at the time.'

Bran catches my eye and mouths 'glass slipper'. I swallow my laugh, because it's not the time for that.

'These dresses are banging, Cindy,' Red exclaims, eyeing a

red mini dress with thin straps and a thigh-high slit. 'Where'd you get them?'

'My mum made them. She is an amazing seamstress and can make just about anything.' Slowly, Cindy takes out the dresses. 'If you each choose one, I can see what adjustments I need to make.'

Bran glares at us. 'I can't believe I'm stuck as a bloody waitress.'

'It was your idea to use the selector app to decide who would get the tickets,' Red replies, holding up the red dress.

'But I didn't think the bloody thing was gonna pick me!'

'Suck it up,' Rap says. 'We have a job to do.'

Rap goes for a black sequinned halter dress with a slit at the front. If Bisi was here, she would choose the mustard off-the-shoulder fishtail dress.

'I'll go with the mustard one,' I say.

Coughing, Maya comes into the living room, bundled up in blankets. 'Mum,' she croaks. 'Where's my dress for the ball?'

Cindy places the back of her hand on Maya's forehead to check her temperature. 'There's no ball for you, not when you're burning up like that, missy.' She taps Maya softly on the bum. 'Go on, back to bed. I'll bring you some lemon and ginger tea for your throat.'

Maya moans, shuffling back to her room. 'I don't want any more of that nasty tea.'

Ding dong.

Dropping her dress, Red answers the door to Giselle. Her voice travels up the stairs.

'Hey, everyone,' Giselle calls. She's rolling a silver suitcase behind her. When Giselle realised that the Assembly had been planning this for some time, she and Red made up.

'How are you, Giselle?' Cindy asks, removing the threaded needle from between her teeth.

'I'm bless,' Giselle replies. 'I've got my mobile business up and running. Best believe I'll be getting my shop back, but this is good for now. So, whose make-up am I doing first?'

'Why don't you try your dresses on?' Cindy asks. 'I can see what amendments I need to make and Giselle can get started.'

I take the mustard dress to the bathroom and wiggle around to get it over my thick thighs. *Don't rip, don't rip, don't rip.* I breathe a sigh of relief as the dress moulds to my body without any problems.

Cindy calls through the locked door. 'Are you decent? Would you like me to zip it up for you?'

'Yes, please.'

Cindy walks in and zips the dress up. 'Oh, you look beautiful, Fola. This colour looks great on you.'

'Thanks, Cindy,' I reply, flipping the skirt with my feet like a mermaid.

Giselle has set up her make-up station on the kitchen table. She starts with my hair, using extensions to create a halo braid so I resemble an angel.

'We're going to keep your foundation light,' Giselle says. 'You have great skin.'

Cindy gushes at us once we're all dressed. 'You all look so beautiful. I hate the idea of leaving you by yourselves to go to the ball, but I can't leave my sick baby alone. I'm glad the doctor said it was just a standard cold and nothing serious. '

'We're going to be fine,' I reassure Cindy—and myself, because our plans rarely go as planned.

'Okay, but if anything happens, call me and I'll come and pick you up straight away.'

Ding dong.

Cindy answers the door. Prince strolls in, tugging at his black bow tie. In his three-piece suit and white shirt, he looks good, especially with the neck tatts popping up by his collar and with his blond hair loose. Priya would die.

'Look at your boy, Fols,' Bran whispers, but her whisper is the same volume as her talking voice.

My face is a furnace. 'Why are you so loud?'

Cindy attempts to hide her smile. 'It's time for you to go now. Don't forget your masks.' She hands them out. 'Please be careful. While you're there, please see if you can knock some sense into my father.'

'I will,' Rap replies.

We discuss the extra part of the plan—the part that Cindy doesn't know about—after we leave her flat.

I shake my bag. 'I need to change.' Prince turns around, blocking me from the rest of the group. Hiking my dress up, I slip on my trousers and trainers.

Rap's black eyeshadow and black lips make her look extra-lethal. 'Why didn't you just put on the dress afterwards?'

'Because Cindy has to think we're going straight to the

ball; not breaking into Rumpel's house,' I reply. 'Aren't you gonna change, Red?'

'Nope. My dress is short enough for me to run in.'

Show off.

Prince laughs.

'I'll find someone who works for Hightower at the ball— maybe they'd want to know about the Assembly's involvement in the mass extermination and displacement of an entire community,' Rap says.

Red asks what we're all thinking. 'But that's not what you're going to start the conversation with, right?'

'Of course, not,' Rap replies. 'I'll greet them and *then* ask them.'

'Alright, this has been fun, but I'm off to pour wine for some rich geezers.' Bran adjusts her black waitress waistcoat and signals to Rap. 'You coming, Rap?'

'I hope that book of yours is real,' Rap says to me. 'It would give us all we need.'

No pressure, then.

'I hope so too,' I reply. 'Let's go.'

Prince, Red and I travel across Folkshore to Rumpelstiltskin's mansion, praying for a miracle.

Keeping to the shadows, we creep around the outside of the mansion and pause at the back window. 'How are we going to get in?' I ask.

'Up there.' Prince points to an open window on the ground floor. 'We need a boost.'

'We can use this,' I say, pointing at a large plant pot in the corner of the garden.

We carry the heavy plant pot and place it under the window. I climb onto the pot, then push the window open wider. As I'm pulling my arms through, someone shoves me and I tumble onto the wooden floor in the kitchen.

'Who pushed me?' I whisper.

Red pulls herself inside next, landing gracefully beside me. 'I did—you were taking too damn long. Do you think we have all day? We're already breaking the law.'

Prince stealthily slips in through the window without messing up his suit.

'I'm surprised Rumpel doesn't have an alarm,' he whispers. 'His collection is worth *millions.*'

At the mention of an alarm, Red turns me. 'Fola, do you know where we're going?'

'Yeah, I think so,' I whisper back, leading them through the dark, quiet mansion. I pause beside the wall that moves like a wave. Eustace spoke about the scroll changing the appearance of everything near it, didn't he? 'I think the book or tablet is in the room behind this.'

Prince pushes the oak door on the wall and it opens easily—too easily. The immense gold room we step into has thick burgundy curtains drawn, allowing only a sliver of light into the room. Glass display cabinets take up most of the room.

'This must be Rumpel's private collection.' Prince whistles at one cabinet in particular. 'It's a late 19th-century hand-painted Meissen pogade. These things go for twelve grand.'

'Twelve what?' Red exclaims.

My phone rings. It's Bran.

'Code red.'

'What?'

'Rumpel-fucking-stiltskin is checking his phone and... now he's leaving!' Bran whispers. *'Did you set off an alarm or something?'*

'Nah, there wasn't one.'

'You ever heard of a silent alarm, Wottie? It doesn't matter. Just find the bloody book and get out of there.'

My heart hammers in my chest at the thought of getting caught and having to deal with Rumpel—or, worse, the police.

'Bran thinks Rumpel is coming back, so we have to find it now and get out,' I say. 'Look for something moving or changing colour.'

We search through the glass cabinets of mirrors, baseball cards, Persian rugs and first editions of books, but the tablet is nowhere to be found.

Then Red gasps.

A cabinet with an old violin inside is beating like a heart.

'It must be close,' I say, checking under the cabinet to see if it's glued under there, but it's not. As Red moves around the cabinet, her heel gets caught in a gap in the hardwood floor.

'No!' Red tugs at her foot.

Coming up behind her, I grab her arms and pull. Prince

drops to the floor, attempting to dislodge her heel. It doesn't budge. Rumpel's car lights beam through the windows, and we freeze.

'Oh shit,' Prince growls. 'Red, I think you're gonna have to leave your shoe behind.'

'What? No!' she cries, tugging at her foot. 'These are my favourites. And if we leave it here, he'll see it.'

'Alright, let's try again. Use all your strength,' I say, swallowing the anxiety creeping up my throat. 'One, two, three, pull!'

The heel slips free and the floorboard shifts, revealing a black object hidden underneath the floor. I reach down and remove the vibrating tablet. *The Chronicles of Folkshore* appears on the screen before it goes blank.

'This is it.'

Rumpel's front door slams shut. 'Who's there?'

We creep through the mansion, scramble through the kitchen window, and fall into a heap in the garden.

'Leave the plant pot,' Red whispers. 'We don't have time!'

We run as far away from Rumpel's house as possible, then stop to catch our breath in a quiet side street.

'We... almost... got... caught,' I wheeze, resting my hand against a wall.

'Who's there?' a police pig grunts, shining her torchlight into the side street. We crouch behind a bin, staying hidden until she trots off into the night. I don't think my heart can take any more.

The tablet pulses in my hands. 'I think it's coming on.'

'Can I see it?' Red asks, taking it from me. 'There are some words on the back. *Say your command.* What's that supposed to—'

The tablet dives out of her hand and hovers in the air. It changes from a scroll to a brown book with golden stitching, and finally to a shimmering orange square.

Prince peers closer. 'What is it?'

'Not a what,' says the orange square in a soft Swedish accent. 'I am the living, breathing history of Folkshore. Now, say your command.'

'Which command?' I whisper. We all stare at the talking square. 'Are you... *The Chronicles of Folkshore*? We don't understand. How do we use you?'

'Help mode initiated,' it says. 'Refer to the directory, where you can find information on any Folkshorian.'

No way.

'Help mode ended. Would you like to go back to the last recorded entry? Say your command.'

'Yes, go back to the last recorded entry,' Red says to the square.

'As you wish,' it responds, transforming into a holographic video.

Prince runs his hands through his blond hair. 'Is that us?'

'It *is* us, but weeks ago, when I came to Folkshore.'

As the holographic video plays, the voice says: '*The Chronicles of Folkshore. At approximately 7:45 Folkshore Standard Time, an unidentified person enters Folkshore with a black bag on their back. This unidentified person is called Fo—*'

The holographic video suddenly transforms back into the orange square.

'The last entry was when I arrived in Folkshore. Why did it stop recording? Was it because of me?'

'Say your command.'

'Who is responsible for everything that's happening?' I ask, with Roland in mind.

'Invalid request.'

'What does "invalid request" mean?' Red snaps, getting impatient. 'Where is Ty? Are the Assembly involved?'

The orange square glows and responds, 'All recorded entries for the Assembly.' The square changes back to the tablet, which drops into my hands. The tablet scrolls through hundreds of video entries that relate to the Assembly, and projects one-second previews of each one.

Something catches my eye. 'Wait! Go back to the entry on the 25th of June.'

The tablet scrolls back, projecting a preview image of Roland in a navy suit grabbing Rumpel's shirt collar.

'I knew it was him!' I shout. 'Play the recorded entry.'

The tablet changes back to the orange square. 'As you wish.' The square changes into another holographic video, but this time it shows Roland and Rumpelstiltskin arguing in an office. As the video plays, Roland releases Rumpel's collar and steps back.

'We had a deal, Roland. I helped you get rid of Duke and become an Assembly member. I endorsed you. You owe me.'

'Feckin' hell,' Prince mutters to himself.

'I made you into who you are today, in exchange for your cooperation. I'm giving you a choice, Roland—either you're with me or against me. There is no in-between.'

'No! I did everything you said,' Roland replies, moving to the other side of the office. 'You don't know how hard I've worked. The regeneration scheme is going well. In a few months, Folkshore will be New Haven. Why don't you just let the rest of the missing people go? You can't keep them down there—I've seen the conditions.'

'The Shriekers have a job to do. They're not done until every single one of them is drained.'

'Why are you working with those... those creatures?'

'The Shriekers and I have a deal. If you play your cards right, you will get something that they never will—freedom.'

The holographic video changes back into a tablet and drops back into my hands. We're all speechless.

It was Rumpel I saw in my vision, not Roland. Why does he need the 'light' so badly? And what is he using it for?

'We need to get to that ball *now*,' Red says.

Chapter 36

We're outside the town hall, where the ball is being held, showing Rap what we found.

'We've got them!' Rap slaps the back of her hand into her palm. 'Rumpelstiltskin isn't back yet, but Roland is in there. The snake. We need to tell him that we know *everything*.'

'Cindy is going to be so upset,' I reply.

'I warned her about her dad. She *has* to listen to me now.'

A woman in a fitted blue dress rushes down the stairs towards us. Quickly, Prince tucks the tablet into his blazer pocket.

'Please say you're Leah,' the woman begs, looking directly at me. 'I'm the party planner and I was told you'd be wearing a... mustard dress.' Her eyes flicker down my outfit.

'Yeah, I am.' I look down and realise that I still have my trousers and trainers on. 'I'll change before I come inside.'

'Be quick. You're late!' she shouts. 'I need you in there right now to take photos.'

'Prince,' I say.

He salutes. 'Aye aye, Princess.' Prince shields me so I can change.

I follow the woman inside, snapping photos along the

way. I use my camera to track members of the Assembly, but there's no sign of Roland yet—or Rumpel.

The town hall's main auditorium has been transformed for this extravagant ball. Candles on the tables illuminate the room. There are gold tablecloths, ceiling drapes and chandeliers—the Assembly are clearly going all out to please the investors. Waiters whisk around the ball with golden trays full of delicious starters.

I take pictures of people in elaborate dresses and creative masks. They probably brought guests in from the 'closed' railway station.

Edward climbs onto the stage. 'It's great to have all of you here. This is the start of something amazing. Drink. Eat. Enjoy.' He raises his champagne glass, saluting the room. 'Raise your glasses to New Haven.'

'New Haven,' the audience cries.

'Psst.' Bran chooses a couple of crab cakes from a tray and balances them in her right hand. 'I've been keeping my nose to the ground, Wottie. The woman in the pink suit that just went to the toilet works for Hightower. I overheard her speaking.'

'Thanks, Sherlock.'

An older white man in a uniform like Bran's approaches us. 'Excuse me, you're not supposed to be eating the hors d'oeuvres,' he says sternly to Bran. 'Those are reserved for guests only.'

'Pipe down. You've been shouting at me all night. You can't eat this, don't do that, stop selling your homemade earrings to the guests. I've had enough.'

I head to the ladies toilets. A willowy black woman in a pink dress is washing her hands at the sink. Shutting off the tap, she dries her hands using one of the small white towels provided before discarding it in the gold wire basket. She turns to face me. 'I was watching you out there—you're a natural. I'm grateful to have such a talented young woman for our event.' The woman offers me her hand. 'My name is Beverly Hart.'

'Leah. Do you work for Hightower?'

She looks at me from under her long eyelashes. 'Yes—what can I do for you?'

'I came here for you—no, that sounds weird. I came here to talk to someone from Hightower.'

Beverly nods and gestures to the velvet sofa along one wall. 'What did you want to speak to me about?'

I maintain eye contact with her. 'You "invested" in Whitemount and it changed. Now, you're "investing" in Folkshore, but do you know what the Assembly and Rumpelstiltskin are up to?'

Beverly folds her hands in her lap. 'It's business. New Haven is another lucrative investment opportunity.'

'Investment opportunity?' I repeat, anger kindling inside me. 'People from Folkshore are being kidnapped and dying—and if you speak up against the Assembly, they try to silence you.'

Beverly's head draws back in surprise. 'And you have proof of these allegations? Hightower seeks to avoid scandals.'

'Yes, we have proof.'

'Tell me more.'

I tell Beverly the whole story and I'm breathless by the end.

She hands me her business card, keeping hold of the other end. 'Call me tomorrow evening. I'll see what I can dig up myself.'

Beverly leaves the toilets. I'm more determined than ever for us to end this. I leave a minute after she does. A familiar figure is lurking behind a pillar. The distinctive grey patch in Roland's black hair makes him recognisable, even though he's wearing a mask.

'We know what you did,' I say.

Roland doesn't seem to recognise me at first, but I lift up my mask briefly then put it back down.

'What are you doing here?' he scowls. 'This ball is strictly invite only.'

'I know why you're scared of Rumpel.'

Roland bristles. 'You don't know what you're talking about.'

'I know that he killed Duke Everbee so you could become an Assembly member.'

'How do you know that?' Roland splutters, looking around to check if anyone is listening to our conversation.

'We also know about the fake regeneration scheme. You knew that Rumpel was kidnapping people.'

Wiping his brow, Roland leans closer. 'Listen, please understand. I didn't know at first, but he has so much on me. He has something on *all* of us.'

'Help us expose him.'

Roland laughs it off. 'Expose Rumpelstiltskin? It's *impossible*. Do you know how hard I've tried to get out from under that man? And you think you are going to help me with my problems? You're just a girl.'

'*Three* girls,' Rap says, appearing to my right. 'And that's more than enough. If it was up to me, you would've been finished already.'

Red appears to my left. 'You're going to release Westley and tell us where my boyfriend, Ty, is.'

'How can I trust you?' Roland asks, his eyes calculating. 'How do I know you're not going to blackmail me with that information too?'

'You don't,' Rap replies, leaning forward with her hand out. 'Do we have a deal?'

Chapter 37

We leave the ball and head back towards Cindy's flat.
'Are you sure we can trust Roland?' Red asks, nervously fiddling with her black clutch bag. 'Do you think he'll take us to the second room?'

'He has no choice,' Rap replies. 'The documentary is out. Everyone is going to be coming for him and the Assembly. He'd better cooperate.'

Black misty shapes form on either side of us. A Shrieker clutches Rap. She swings her fist at it, but it goes right through the dark mist. Stretching out a shadowy arm, another Shrieker brandishes a dagger and slashes it in my direction. I duck.

'Stop!' I yell at the group of Shriekers. 'Rumpelstiltskin is lying to you. There's no freedom. You can't be set free!'

They don't stop.

A Shrieker corners Red, the metal device dangling from its claws. I use my heel to stab at it. Darkness blows away like wind.

'Use your phones!' I shout, staggering into the road.

A rough hand snatches my arm, locking it behind my

back. I don't know who's behind me, but their breath tickles the hairs on my neck.

'I think it's time we had that little talk,' Rumpelstiltskin says before something hard hits the side of my head.

I flinch.

'The next station is Brixton. Change for National Rail services. This station has step-free access.'

I peel open my eyes. I'm in Folkshore station, and a train sits beside me on the platform. Handcuffs dig into my wrist. I'm chained to a chair. My mustard dress is torn at the hem and my feet are covered in dirt.

Rumpel stands in front of me with a small vial of Lx20. Light. He pulls down his surgical mask, examining the vial. 'It's a beauty, isn't it?'

There's a ping-pong match going on in my chest. 'What am I doing here?'

'Ah-ah, we're jumping ahead. The mole hasn't yet been buried.' Rumpel strolls towards the edge of the platform, his hands in his trouser pockets as he gazes at Folkshore's skyline. 'What a beauty. I'll have control over Folkshore soon. I can taste it.'

Endless sparks of blue lightning from the Hometree connect with the sky, creating a tiny black hole above Folkshore. It's exactly like in my vision. I know what comes next.

'You don't have control! Can't you see that you're killing Folkshore and poisoning everyone? The report—'

'I know about the report.' Rumpel faces me, a sympathetic smile on his face. 'While those fools laughed at it, I consumed that report, testing the soil and the people with the handy device I created.' The metal device dangles from Rumple's hand.

'But why? I don't understand. Why did you need the light?'

'Think, Fola,' he says.

He knows my name.

'I needed to break Folkshore and the hold Folkshorians have over it.' He leans close to my face, and my words dry up. 'The light controls everything. If I can control the light, I can control Folkshore.'

'But... but the light is in everything. How can you —'

Rumpel groans in frustration. 'If I drain Folkshore enough...if I drain *enough* of the land and its people, then Folkshore won't be controlled by *anything*. It can be controlled by me and I can do what needs to be done. Folkshore has so much potential. New Haven is its future.'

The blue lightning from the Hometree crackles and explodes, widening the black hole enough for smaller items to be sucked inside.

'The light is Folkshore's life-source. There won't be any Folkshore left for you to control,' I say. 'What do you want from me?'

'When you stepped into Folkshore, the tablet stopped showing me what I needed to know. Why is that?'

'What tablet?'

'I know you have it. I let you take it,' he reveals, making me feel stupid for thinking we outsmarted him. 'I thought maybe it would start recording again, since you're the reason it stopped in the first place. If you tell me, I'll let you leave on this train.'

'Please.' Vomit shoots up my throat and out of my mouth, splattering down my dress. 'I don't know why it stopped. I just want to go home to my family... to my brother. He's sick. I'm not supposed to be here.' Tears fill my eyes, but I don't let them go.

'I can work with this.' Rumpel mutters to himself. 'How about you tell me where the tablet is and why it stopped? I'll let you go home on this train.'

He's giving me what I want, but I can't give him what he wants.

Rumpel senses my hesitation. 'Didn't you say your brother was sick? You don't really know how long he has left, do you?' Rumpel grabs my cheeks between his hands, squeezing tightly. 'If you can't give me what I want, you're of no use to me. Your documentary and the protest won't work either.'

A shriek echoes down the platform, but no vision comes this time, only pain. The Shrieker's misty body shifts near me, securing the metal device to my chest.

'Please! Please. Don't do this.'

The cold metal pierces my skin, causing a numbing pain.

Energy drains from my body, but I know I mustn't fall asleep. Voices swarm in my head. Priya's, Mum's and finally, Deji's.

'Fols.'

'Omowafola.'

'Fola. Sis. Wake up.'

'Enough!' Rumpel roars, tearing the device out of my chest. My blood splatters over the platform. Then his phone rings, causing the Shrieker to squeal in pain.

Rumpel answers quickly. 'What are you blathering on about? Everyone is doing what? This is expected, but you must stick to the plan.' Rumpel chucks the metal device to the platform floor. 'Take her away.'

Officer Levi appears in front of me with his usual sneer. 'You're going to end up just like your friend, Ty.'

'What did you do to Ty?' I ask, struggling against Officer Levi as he unlocks the handcuffs from the seat and drags me down the platform. 'What happened to him?'

Officer Levi chuckles and doesn't reply. I stumble along, my feet completely numb. Officer Levi moves his hoof along the glass panelling like Prince did weeks ago and hits the centre to reveal the steps down into the tunnels.

'In you get,' he spits. 'And don't try anything funny.'

I climb down the stairs, back into the tunnels that I know so well. We head towards the rooms under the station, where Bran and Prince were kept. Officer Levi opens the metal door, shoving me into the room. I hold on to the table in the centre of the room and the door closes behind me.

I need to get out of here.

My gaze locks on to the air vent in the corner of the room. If the blueprints are correct, the air vent should lead to a ventilation system, and I should be able to escape through the tunnels. Removing the vent cover, I squeeze myself through.

Chapter 38

I burst out through the manhole on Enchanted Square. Folkshore is in complete chaos. All the trees I can see are alight with the same blue lightning as the Hometree.

'We. Are. Folkshore!' Rap calls through a megaphone, standing on the Rapunzel statue.

'We are Folkshore!' the protestors repeat.

'They think they can get away with this. But. We. Won't. Let. Them!'

The police hover on the edge of the crowd. One trots forward with their own megaphone.

'Everyone supporting this—'

'No, no, we won't go!'

'We will shut this down—'

'No, no, we won't go.'

'This is your last warning—'

'NO, NO, WE WON'T GO!'

There's a thunderous cry as the protestors push against the police, who are possessed both with power and the divisive toxins in the air, causing them to go into a frenzy—just like the report said. Batons slam against flesh, and gas canisters are thrown into the crowd. Instead of dispersing, the crowd get angrier. They fight back. Folkshore is at war with itself and its people.

As if on cue, ear-piercing shrieks clash with the shouts of the crowd and the crackle of lightning from the sky. Shriekers appear, picking people off in the crowd. One shrieks directly in my face. Without my phone, I'm defenceless against it.

Covering my ears, I dive between its legs, but it grabs my ankle, sending a searing pain through my leg.

'Let her go!' Bran shouts, bringing her blaring phone to its ear.

It shrieks in pain.

'Everyone! Ringtones! Now!' Rap hollers through the megaphone. There's a blend of ringtones, crippling the Shriekers.

I jump to my feet and hug Bran. She squeezes me back.

'Wottie, where've you been? We found Ty and Anna in the second room.'

So Roland kept his word—at least one thing is going as it should.

The blue lightning shooting from the Hometree crackles fiercely and intensifies, sending an extra-powerful surge of energy into the sky.

'I'll tell you about it later. We're running out of time. Find the rest of the group!'

'Why?'

'We need to get some of the white light back into the

Hometree. It won't reverse anything, but we need to restore the balance somehow. The Hometree is the centre.' I rush through the protestors, dodging the Shriekers and police pigs. If I'm right, the out-of-order water hydrant by the Hometree is connected to the water tank through the pipes. The tank was full of white light. I drop to the ground a few metres away from the Hometree, and crawl around to find the maintenance hatch. My trainer falls off and it's sucked up by the black hole.

I lift up the small door and remove one of the long rubber hosepipes. I tighten it around my waist and take out a second hosepipe, attaching one end of the pipe to the nozzle on the water hydrant. I twist the valve at the top, but it's rusted shut.

'Step away from that—or else,' Officer Levi threatens, slapping the baton against his hoof. 'Rumpelstiltskin said you'd be here, but I didn't think you'd be that smart. Now, I won't ask you again. Step away.'

'No, *you* step away,' Rap says, holding a police baton in her hands. She is with Red, Prince and Officer Kelly.

'You snake!' Officer Levi shouts as they advance towards him.

'What do you need?' Prince asks, kneeling beside me.

'You need to twist the value open while I get close enough to the Hometree.'

'I'll hold the end of the hosepipe for you,' Rap offers. 'I can't have you getting sucked into the black hole. It'll be an inconvenience.'

I crack a smile.

Rap holds onto the end of the hosepipe wrapped around my waist. I grab the other pipe connected to the water hydrant and battle the pull of the black hole as I near the Hometree.

'Prince, twist now!'

The wind rushes in my ears.

'Nothing's coming, princess!' Prince yells over the chaos.

Wasn't my theory right?

I look up as the Hometree crackles, sparking more blue lightning threads into the sky, widening the black hole further.

My body becomes airborne. I scream as I'm pulled towards the black hole in the sky, but a hard tug on the hose-pipe halts my body.

'You can't get away from us that easy, Wottie!' Bran shouts.

Rap, Bran, Cindy, and Red hold onto the end of the hose-pipe like in a game of tug-of-war.

My feet land on the ground.

'Prince, look around. We're missing something.' He scrambles about, trying to find the issue.

'Found it!' Prince exclaims, pointing at a lever a few metres away from the water hydrant.

With death literally looming over us, Prince pumps the lever with all his strength, building up the pressure until the white light from the pipes below begins to flow through the water hose.

'It's workin.'

'It's working,' I repeat, almost crying as I grab the end of the hose and stick it into the soil under the Hometree. As the soil absorbs the liquid, the lightning around the Hometree's sparks erratically, making us all jump back.

I cover my ears as a uniform squeal from all the Shriekers echoes across Enchanted Square. A Shrieker is pulled into the air and the rest of the Shriekers follow, creating a sinister, pulsing, shadowy ball in the sky. Nothing happens for a few seconds, then the dark cloud is dragged by an unknown force into the ground, where it disappears.

The black hole in the sky begins to shrink and close up. The Hometree crackles once more with sparks of blue lightning before glowing a magnificent white.

Silence settles over Folkshore.

Chapter 39

The hands on the hospital clock are moving the wrong way, slowing down time even further.

'Are there any updates on my nephew?' Mal asks, hovering by Dr Ida.

Dr Ida shakes her head. 'I'm very sorry, Mal. He's still in a Sleeping Beauty coma.'

Red snores on my shoulder and Rap leans on the wall opposite us, staring into space.

Dani is curled in Cindy's lap and Maya is slumped in a chair, sleeping. I stand, stretching my legs, and Red shifts to sleep the other way.

As I walk outside, the crisp breeze hits me and I savour it, breathing in the fresh Folkshore air. The sound of a car door slamming disrupts the silence. It's a pale woman in a black suit, exiting a blue Mercedes.

'Ms Fola Oduwole,' she says.

I've been waiting for her.

The Assembly's trial is this afternoon. A neutral mediator was called to oversee the case and has taken statements from everyone involved. The woman in the Mercedes is the mediator. She's called Sawyer Madden. I've spoken to her already, but she scheduled a last-minute interview with me before the trial. She hands me a red textured card with an address on it. 'Your presence is required today at the Galadriel Building.'

'Thanks,' I reply, taking the card.

'No, thank you for your cooperation, Fola. See you soon.' Sawyer gets back into the car and drives away from the hospital.

'What did she want?' Prince asks. He's leaning against the wall behind me, smoking.

'I thought you quit.'

Shrugging, Prince asks again, 'What did she want?'

I show him the card in my palm before responding. 'An extra last-minute interview.'

'Why?' Prince questions. 'You've already been.'

'Sawyer likes to be thorough,' I reply, mentally counting down the minutes until this will all be over. 'The interview is at the Galadriel Building. Do you know where it is?'

Prince grins, ruffling his hair. 'Yeah. I'll be your tour guide, for old times' sake.'

The Galadriel Building is off Enchanted Square. A guard opens the door as we approach, ushering us through a full body scanner.

'Do we really need all of this?' I grumble.

The guard ignores me and Prince chuckles.

Several lime-green doors line the corridor, like in a game show. Sawyer stands outside the second door on the left. 'Ms Oduwole. Thanks for coming. Your friend can wait here.' She leads me through the door into a cosy room with two lime-green armchairs.

'Why don't you take a seat, Fola?' Sawyer says. Her dark eyes crinkle at the corners. I sink into the armchair, clinging to the arms as Sawyer sits in the chair opposite and takes out a recorder.

'Why don't we start from the beginning?' Sawyer asks, crossing her legs. 'How did you get into Folkshore?'

'Haven't I answered these questions before?' I ask, confused. 'What is this really about?'

Sawyer grins, knowing she's been caught out. She leans forward to pause the recorder. 'We've found out some new information about a tablet that was in Rumpelstiltskin's possession, but the tablet is currently missing. Do you know where I can find this tablet?'

'No.'

'Is that your final answer, Ms Oduwole?' Sawyer asks, leaning forward in her chair.

'Yup.'

Shaw fixes her gaze on me before starting the recorder again. 'Let's run through your last encounter with Rumpelstiltskin Gold.'

Folkshorians pack the auditorium for the sentencing of the Assembly and Rumpel.

Sawyer has finished her investigations, which paint a sad picture of what happened here in Folkshore. The judge they brought in for this case signals for the side door to be opened. One by one the Assembly members step out. Folkshorians boo them. Then Rumpel steps out. Someone throws a shoe at his head, but he ducks at the last minute.

The judge bashes her wooden gavel a few times. 'Order!'

The auditorium quietens down.

Roland bows his head.

'This is the most ashamed I've ever seen him,' Cindy says, anger in her voice.

'A conspiracy charge is being brought against the Assembly. You knowingly reached an agreement with Rumpelstiltskin Gold to allow outsiders into Folkshore for your own monetary gain. Exposure of *any* hidden place is a crime. However, we have considered your statements and evidence of coercion by Mr Gold. You have also cooperated with our case against Mr Gold. And you have all pleaded guilty.'

Rumpel seethes in his chair.

'Rumpelstiltskin Gold. You are being charged with the murder of Duke Everbee, manslaughter, extortion...'

Chapter 40

Enchanted Square is covered in flowers, pictures and burning candles as we gather by the Hometree. Alice stands by us, mourning her father and the others lost. Cindy huddles beside Leonard, who rests on his cane.

Rap addresses the crowd, Westley by her side. 'Mourn the deaths of those brutally taken away, but also celebrate their lives.'

The memorial plaque reveals the extent of the damage Rumpelstiltskin and the Assembly caused.

IN MEMORY OF THOSE
WHOSE LIVES WERE TAKEN

ESMERELDA RUBIO — AGE 32
ARTHUR SIDIBE — AGE 86
ANASTASIA BALOGUN — AGE 15
BAMBI MICHAELS — AGE 10
ROSE BOATENG — Age 67
ROBIN CHOI — AGE 25
ARIEL LEVI — AGE 13
BRIAR WÄNG — AGE 5
FINN DAVANI — AGE 21
PASCAL MONTGOMERY — AGE 38
TYRONE WOLFE CAMPBELL — AGE 17

The list goes on. I wipe tears from my face, holding Red with one arm and Bran with the other. Red crouches, placing a photo of Ty in one of his grey hoodies in front of the memorial.

'It's okay, baby,' Red's mum says as Red runs into her arms, sobbing.

As soon as Folkshore was safe again, Red's parents flew back from Jamaica. Folkshore will never be the same, but I know the Folkshorians will stick together.

Jackie comes up beside us, sniffling into a scrunched tissue, and clutches Bran's hand. 'I've got you.'

'Are you ready to go, sweetie?' Cindy asks, reminding me of my own reality. 'Your train leaves soon.'

I nod, taking one last look at the plaque. Despite what they're going through, the group gathers to walk me to the station. I've wanted to leave Folkshore for a long time, but I didn't think I'd be leaving like this.

We stand on the platform, watching people board the train to main London.

Bran pulls me into a hug and I squeeze her back. 'Message me, Wottie.'

'I will, Sherlock.'

I don't need to say anything to Red, we just hug, and I move on to Cindy.

'I promised myself that I wouldn't cry,' Cindy says, crying. 'I'm going to miss you so much, sweetie. Here's a gift from the girls.' She stuffs Dani's drawings in my hand, and Maya's official business card.

Rap nods. 'Laters, Fola. I'll message you the details.'

Rap's organising a surprise birthday dinner for Red, which I'm the official photographer for. I know Red doesn't feel like doing anything, but she deserves a nice birthday.

'The next station is Brixton. Change for National Rail services. This station has step-free access.'

Prince shoulders his black duffle bag and steps onto the train with me.

Behind Prince's back, Bran winks at me before making the 'OK' hand gesture. 'Do *everything* I would do.'

I'm going to miss her, but she's still annoying. The train doors beep and slam shut, separating me from my second family. I wave to them on the platform as the train darts forward, throwing me back into my seat.

Prince fusses with something in his duffle bag.

'You didn't bring the tablet, did you?' I ask nervously.

'I gave it to Alice,' he replies, zipping up his bag properly. 'This is a framed drawing for Noah. I can't wait to see him.' Looking deep in thought, Prince rubs his thumb over his tally tattoo.

'I guess you won't be adding to it, then.'

When we reach Brixton, all the missed calls and messages come through to my phone at once. The time switches back to normal. I've been gone for two days.

Deji

> Fola. How's the trip?
>
> Hey
>
> What are you doing?
>
> Priya told me what you did!!!
>
> Since when were you a risk taker?
>
> Hope you're good though.
>
> I didn't tell Mum and Dad
>
> Going in for surgery

Priya

> You're online!!!!
>
> Where have you been????

Me

> You'll think I'm lying

Priya

> Where are you?
>
> I covered for you. I told Ms Jackson that you were sick and your parents that the trip was extended. You owe me.

Me

> Thank you so much

> I'm still in London. I'm going to see Deji, but I'll call you later.

'Everything alright?' Prince asks, nudging my shoulder.

'Yeah, my friend covered for me.'

'The next station is Euston. Doors will open on the right-hand side. Change for London Overground and National Rail services.'

I grip the bar and stand up. 'This is my stop. Don't forget our revision session next Friday.'

'Grand.' Prince leans in for a hug and whispers, 'I hope your brother's surgery went okay.'

'Me too,' I whisper back.

Deji's surgery was hours ago. He should be in recovery. I rush out of Euston station and run towards the hospital. I don't take a proper breath until I'm in the lift. I reach Deji's room in record time, almost colliding with the doctor leaving.

'Sorry,' I say. 'Is my brother alright? Did his surgery go well?'

He kind of looks like Dr Eric, but I hope he's nothing like him.

'You must be Fola,' he replies, flashing a Hollywood smile. 'Yes, your brother's surgery went *very* well, but he needs time to recover. Deji will need all of your support.'

All the tension that has built up inside me over the last few weeks vanishes. 'Thank you, thank you, thank you.'

Deji is asleep in his hospital bed. I drag a chair up to his bed, making sure I don't disturb any wires.

'Fola.' Deji shifts sluggishly in his bed. 'What... happened?'

'You'll never believe me. I got trapped in this place called Folkshore.'

'Folkshore? That... place... not... real.'

'It is! I swear on Mum's life,' I reply, tucking his hand back under the hospital sheets. 'The animals talk there.'

Slowly, Deji turns his head. 'You... took some... of... my morphine.'

My heart feels heavy as I remember being in hospital with Pascal before his condition got worse.

'And I met some of the best people.' I don't say anything else for a long time. Instead, I listen to Deji breathing, thankful that he's still here.

Epilogue

Five Months Later

Folkshore changed my life. I know I sound dramatic, but it did. When I got back and I knew that Deji was alright, I focused on the things that most mattered to me.

When Gregg mentioned the Charlton Film Festival competition again, I knew what I had to do. He helped me find a team for my short film, but nothing could ever beat the team I had in Folkshore.

The short film I wrote and directed won first place!

'You should dedicate the film to me,' Deji says, fixing his tie. 'You know, since entering the competition was my idea.'

Mum's gele blocks my view. 'Mum, seriously. You didn't have to dress up.'

'Do you think I'm going to wear jeans when my eldest daughter's film won?' Mum announces, adjusting her head tie in the front mirror. 'Hollywood will be calling your name soon.'

Beside me, Bisi rolls her eyes. 'Hollywood? Mum, it's just a festival. But it's still cool, though.'

I know it kills Bisi to compliment me.

'You know, I've always wanted to write a film about my life,' my dad says with a calm smile.

Roti nudges me, making a 'what are they on?' face. I laugh and shrug.

'Oya, come and snap my picture, Fola.' Mum poses in front of the car outside the festival venue.

'Dad, can you step closer to Mum?' I ask.

My dad's wearing his blue agbada with pride. It matches Mum's iro and buba. Roti is stuffed—by force—into his 'special suit'. Bisi has on her favourite peach bodycon dress, and Deji is wearing the biggest smile.

'Everyone say "cheese",' I sing as I take a few shots. 'Okay, let's go. I don't wanna be late.'

Mum fixes her gele again, frowning. 'They should be able to wait for the celebrant.'

'Celebrant? Mum, it's not my birthday.'

'Fola, you must claim it,' Mum replies, shaking her finger at me. 'You're the head, not the tail.'

I hear a scream before I see Priya.

'You look amazing!' she squeals. '*Definitely* the right choice.'

I smooth down my mustard dress. 'Thanks.'

'Hi, Mr and Mrs Oduwole. Did I say it right this time?'

'You tried,' my mum says, pursing her lips.

The festival coordinator takes us right to the front to sit down. I can't stop myself gazing around in awe.

'Welcome to the Charlton Film Festival.'

There's a round of applause from the audience.

'We're joined today by some of the most talented young people from across the country. Our film competition had the most entries this year. We think it's so important that we're providing opportunities for everyone. The film industry lacks diversity, and we strive to give a platform to those unheard voices. Now, without further ado, here's the winning film, by Fola Oduwole.'

The opening credits come up. *Finding Your Way Home*. It's a short film about a young Nigerian girl lost in London looking for her parents. She only has Polaroids as clues to where they might be.

When it's my turn to stand up and give a speech, I wobble slightly in my heels, praying I don't end up falling on my face. 'Thank you so much. To be honest, I never thought I'd win this competition. Months ago, when my teacher told me about it, I had already made up my mind that I wouldn't enter. I thought, "What's the point?" This film is very close to my heart, and I couldn't have done it without my community. Over the past few months, I have truly figured out what community means: it's not just about the area you live in, but about the people you surround yourself with. It's the people you call friends and family. The people who are willing to do the most for you and to fight for you. I dedicate this to communities everywhere, and to my brother. I have the best...'

Dani waves at me from the back of the room. *What is she doing here?*

Cindy hollers, 'Keep going, sweetie!'

The whole group is here. They all came for me.

'I have the best community. Thank you.'

I get a standing ovation.

All I can think about are my friends. The festival ends and I move towards the back of the room as quickly as I can. Priya follows me.

'Isn't that the cute boy from the night tour?' she asks, spotting Prince. 'Hey, what haven't you told me?'

Cindy wraps me up in the biggest hug, and I feel like I'm back in Folkshore again.

'You look so beautiful, honey,' she says. 'Congrats again. You deserve all of it.'

'You look banging,' Red remarks before hugging me.

'Oi oi! Sexy Wottie—I've missed you.'

'I missed you too, Sherlock.'

Rap nods, lingering behind the others. Prince's hands rest on the shoulders of the cutest curly-haired boy.

'Noah, I'd like you to meet Fola. Fola, meet Noah.'

Noah waves at me and I wave back.

Crouching down, I give Maya and Dani hugs too. I've missed them, especially my big scammer.

'Aren't you going to introduce us?' Priya asks, her eyes focused on Prince.

'Yeah. This is Prince—'

'Hi!' Priya blurts, a dreamy look in her eyes.

'Guys, meet my best friend, Priya.'
'I thought I was your bestie, Wottie!' Bran shouts.
'We'll fight,' Priya jokes and we all laugh.
I hope Bran knows it's a joke.

THE END

Acknowledgments

I started writing this book in 2018 and it was my first ever complete novel. *Finding Folkshore* is truly my first born and I'm so proud of how the book has turned out.

I want to start off, always, by thanking God because He helps me with my ideas and when I'm struggling, so thank you!

Thank you to Cherise Lopes-Baker because you were as excited about *Finding* as I was and you were the best editor. Thank you to Daquan Cadogan for stepping in as my editor and for picking up where Cherise left off. Thanks to copy-editor Jane Hammett for tightening everything up! I also want to thank the rest of the Jacaranda team for all your hard work on this book: Noemi, Kamillah, Tiffany and Niki.

I must thank my first ever critique partners, Tomi and Amy, because you really saw Finding in its first sorry state. Your feedback was invaluable and apologies for the mess I sent.

Thank you to Jodi-Ann Johnson and Jinny Alexander for sensitivity reading!

To my early readers, Lydia Martindale and Joanna Martindale, I really appreciate you and your great reviews.

Thank you to my family (Tope, Mark, Mum and Dad) for always championing and supporting me ever since the beginning.

To Debs and Mariam, thanks for cheering me on! And to Yasmin Samengo-Turner, after all of those Wagamama dates, Finding Folkshore finally exists!

And to anyone else who I've forgotten, thank you!

About the Author

Rachel Faturoti is an author, screenwriter and poet with a passion for broadening the scope of authentic Black representation in fiction. Rachel released her debut children's novel, *Sadé and Her Shadow Beasts*, in 2022.